Violet

CHRIS KENISTON

Indie House Publishing

Indie House Publishing

BOOKS BY CHRIS KENISTON

Hart Land
Heather
Lily
Violet
Iris
Hyacinth

Farraday Country
Adam
Brooks
Connor
Declan
Ethan
Finn
Grace
Hannah
Ian
Jamison
Keeping Eileen

Aloha Series Heartwarming Edition
Aloha Texas
Almost Paradise
Mai Tai Marriage
Dive Into You
Look of Love
Love by Design
Love Walks In
Flirting with Paradise

Surf's Up Flirts
(Aloha Series Companions)
Shall We Dance
Love on Tap
Head Over Heels
Perfect Match
Just One Kiss
It Had to Be You

**Other Books
By Chris Keniston**

Honeymoon Series
Honeymoon for One
Honeymoon for Three

Family Secrets Novels
Champagne Sisterhood
The Homecoming
Hope's Corner

Original Aloha Series
Waikiki Wedding

ACKNOWLEDGEMENTS

This is the fun part of writing books, where I get to recognize and thank all the people who have helped me along the road to writing a story.

Violet proved challenging for a couple of reasons. For making it so much easier I have to thank the fabulous author Dale Mayer for knowing so much more about... stuff (no spoilers allowed LOL) than I do! And of course the lovely author Barb Han for knowing all about yoga, and for my dear friend author Linda Steinberg for suggesting I join her for yoga on Tuesday afternoons! It all helps!

Once again the delicious recipe included is thanks to my aunt Mary, she's a lifesaver!

I know there are so many more people to thank who keep me going when I'm slow on ideas or struggling to meet deadlines, but it would be impossible to thank them all on the written page, so I'll settle for a thank you to all the wonderful people in my life who make everything easier for me!

Enjoy!

"I don't see it working."
"Not you too?"
"Once is lucky. Twice could be coincidence. Three times…"
"Requires skill. Which we have. You'll see."

CHAPTER ONE

S crambling to fit one more project into his already stretched to the limit schedule, the last thing Grant Whitaker needed was delays from a downpour to rival Hurricane Hilda.

The truck's speakers sounded an incoming call and without thinking he tapped the steering wheel to answer. "Whitaker."

"You staying dry?" his grandfather asked.

"Doing my best. How about you?"

"Your Grandmother didn't marry a fool. I know a good time to settle in with the sports channels." Low chatter from the television announcers hummed in the background. "Don't suppose you've found a good woman to keep you home?"

Grant opted to ignore the not so subtle jab at his bachelorhood. "On my way to a construction site. The retirement village. Phase one is ready for finishes. Phase two is framed and presales for the independent living have gone so well we're moving the groundbreaking up for the memory care unit."

"It was pretty smart of you to build the commercial side first. Most folks would have built the housing then added the shops."

"Where's the fun in doing things the way most people do it?" That was a phrase his grandfather had used so often in his life that it was a standing joke with the entire family.

His grandfather chuckled. "Won't get an argument out of me.

Have you reached out to the General yet?"

"I've tried. For a retired man, he keeps himself hard to reach."

"That would be retired *general*. Sitting still isn't anything they do well. You didn't give up, did you?"

"No. I took your advice. Made reservations at the lake. I agree, deals like this are better fleshed out in person." Which was one of the reasons Grant was good at what he did. In a modern world of online meetings and texts, he understood the value of face to face contact. He'd been taught long ago that the best deals of his career would be made on the golf course. Same could be said over a cup of hot chocolate at a lakeside cabin. "It's why I'm driving in this mess. In order to carve out a couple of days I needed to bump a few things up on my schedule."

"Sounds good, but stay safe and when you get there, let me know if I should book your grandmother and me a cabin. I've heard a lot of nice things about Hart Land."

"Will do. Give Mums my love."

The call disconnected and Grant smiled to himself. His grandfather had taught him everything he knew about business long before Grant truly understood what was happening. If his grandfather's lead about the Hart Land was spot on, rearranging his plans to clear time to visit Retired Marine Corps General Harold Hart would be worth spending a few hours today impersonating a drowning rat. Every developer in the northeast knew the Hart family owned the single largest section of undeveloped waterfront land on popular Lake Lawford. Grant didn't need his Harvard degree to know this next deal could be the coup of the decade. The largest planned resort community in decades.

Through the sheets of rain, he slowed to spot the dirt road that led to the main construction site. It had taken two years to pull this not so little project off. At almost every turn the investors doubted his vision. Even his partner, Joe Fiorello, had bucked him on building commercial space first. In three states, Fiorello Construction might be the most recognizable name whenever a new building goes up, but it was Grant's eye for a deal and gift for making it happen that had put F&W Development Co. on the world map.

Despite sitting nearly a foot off the ground in his quad cab pickup, the pot holes from the large trucks hauling earth up and down this path had him rattling around like a kid at a birthday party bounce house. At least he knew a well-worn rut in the road meant that despite the weather's uncooperative nature, the work for the new phase was well underway.

"Hey, Mr. Whitaker. What brings you here on a day like today?" The security guard popped his head out of the small booth at the gate. The days when a construction site of this size could go unfenced were long gone. At this stage of the game a human face had to be added to the loss prevention plans.

"Just popping in for a quick check."

"Mr. Fiorello was here earlier this morning." A construction man to the bone, Joe could work through a typhoon if needed. Though Grant had no idea what would need him out here on a day like today.

"You stay dry, Jeff."

"Will do. You too." The man slid the glass window shut.

Thanks to the torrential downpour, the crew all toiled at the finishing work on the first condos. The man he wanted to check on would be in the office trailer. As soon as the rain stopped they'd be able to move out of the trailer and into the facilities office for the new maintenance building. The building at the rear of the compound would be used for storage as well. An extra layer of security. With little activity on this end of the site, and only the new site supervisor's truck in front, he parked his pickup near the entrance. A fresh gust of wind helped shove the narrow door wide open, blowing him and the rain inside.

"Grant?" Larry looked up, eyes brimming with surprise. "Didn't expect to see you here."

"Yeah, well." He shook off as much of the drenching as he could and walked over to the work table, leaving a trail of droplets in his wake. "I've got to head up north for a few days. This is the only time I could squeeze in coming by. How are you settling in?"

"Fine, thanks." The supervisor cast a quick glance out the window then back. No doubt thinking the same thing Grant did—what the hell did he think he could do on a day like today?

"The investors are all over me like white on rice. I've never seen such a jittery bunch. I need this next phase to go off without a hitch."

Not even the dollar signs from hefty presales could squash the complaints of building too much too fast.

"Yeah," Larry nodded, "I heard."

Grant looked up from perusing the plans sprawled open on the table. Why had Larry heard? Grant was the only contact with the investors. Joe handled the construction and Grant handled the suits, having just enough interaction with the work sites to keep abreast.

"Something wrong?" Larry asked.

"No." Grant brushed off his concerns. Of course Larry knew about the investors. Even though he'd kept his reports to Joe at a minimum to avoid making his partner any more doubtful about the pace of this project then he already was, the PITA investors wasn't a secret. Especially with Larry; the guy had been supervisor on dozens of projects through the years and knew the business almost as well as he and Joe. Had saved their butts on this one, shifting projects at the last minute. "Should have had more coffee this morning."

The foreman moved from where he'd been standing next to Larry, filled a travel mug and handed it to Grant. "Fresh pot."

"Thanks." He practically inhaled the first long hot gulp. Definitely the elixir of the gods. How did anyone survive a work day without coffee? He loved watching a project grow from drawing to turn key. And F&W provided the epitome of turn key. The best quality guaranteed. And they charged for it too. "Are we still running ahead of schedule for the main building?"

Larry nodded. "Told Joe we should be delivering about two weeks early."

The size of his best supervisor's grin was no surprise. There were hefty bonuses for everyone if a project came in early. Grant believed in spreading the windfall around and every crew member knew it. He walked over to the tiny window in the trailer. From here all he could see was the excavation. "How far behind on phase three will this weather put us?"

"Hard to say. If the squall doesn't stall we'll be fine. If it sits over us for a few days, well, you know how that goes."

"Yeah." Phase one had gone surprisingly well despite the shift in supervisors. He'd never known a project not to run into a snafu of some sort and this particular project seemed to be running almost too good to be true. Maybe his luck was about to run out.

● ● ● ●

"Namaste. And that's it for today." Violet clicked on the remote control, fading the music to silence.

"Will we still be here next week?" one of the two women in the class asked.

Pushing to her feet, the other woman shook her head. "I hope not. I never realized how spoiled I was having a yoga studio only a short walk from my apartment."

Boy, did Violet know that. In the time since her yoga studio had flooded, one by one, almost all her regular clients had found an excuse to skip class at her temporary location. She'd never realized how much of her customer base was due to convenience and not a reflection on her. "It doesn't sound like the old studio will be ready as quickly as I had hoped."

The first lady nodded, but her expression didn't look any more happy about the news than the other woman's.

"Perhaps I'll postpone classes until further notice." She wished the two ladies didn't look so pleased with that announcement. "You can continue to stretch on your own and as soon as we're up and running again I'll send out notifications."

Grinning from ear to ear, the ladies bobbed their heads and gathered their belongings. Violet hoped silently that by the time the studio was open again she still had a client base and wouldn't have to start her business from scratch.

"See you soon," the shorter blonde waved.

"We hope," the other woman added.

A towel in one hand, Violet forced a smile and waved with her free hand. Her mat rolled up and her belongings somewhat neatly tucked in her bag, she looked around the place and wondered now what? Mrs. Renfru was *what.* The building owner had not uttered a word in over a week. Giving the woman her space to deal with a difficult situation was one thing, but it was definitely time for Violet to speak up. After all, if she needed to find a new permanent location, the sooner the better.

Scrolling through her contacts in search of Renfru, the phone buzzed and the screen lit up with the landlady's name. Maybe the universe was finally on her side. "Hello, Mrs. Renfru."

"Hello, Violet. You always sound so nice and relaxed."

"Thank you." She'd worked hard most of her life to not allow the chaos of a busy city like Boston to steal her peace. Despite the upbeat words, something in her landlady's tone left Violet unsure that right now she'd be able to win that particular battle. "What news do you have?"

"I'm afraid it's not good."

Oh, how Violet hated it when her gut instinct and her peace of mind collided.

"It seems that after the water cleanup, the company found traces of mold."

Alarm bells rang loud and clear in Violet's ear.

"Enough that they had to call in someone to test. That's what's been taking so long."

Nothing about this woman's tone of voice was reassuring.

"All the ground floor space affected by the flood needs to have mold remediation. Thankfully that much is actually covered by my insurance policy. At least most of it."

Okay, Violet felt some of the tension in her shoulders ease. That wasn't as bad as she had braced herself for.

"But not the electrical."

"Electrical?"

"The water damaged some of the wiring. The insurance will cover the damaged wiring but according to the electrician's estimate, once he touches any of the wiring, he's required to bring the entire building up to code."

And the other shoe came crashing down with the full weight of Jack's giant.

"I simply can't afford to do that. Not to mention once we start opening up walls, who knows what else they'll find. Without the updates the city won't issue a certificate of occupancy for the retail spaces."

"No." Hands full, Violet sank to the floor in a butterfly pose. "I can see where that's a problem."

"I need the rental income. I can't—won't—raise the tenants' rents enough to offset the losses."

Thank heaven for that. Violet's rent hadn't gone up in all the years she'd lived in Mrs. Renfru's building. Though she suspected it was because of what she paid for the studio.

"I'm considering selling the building."

And that would be a locked and loaded guarantee of her rents for both the apartment and the studio skyrocketing.

"My only other option is a loan from the bank, but frankly I don't know if that will work for me. I'm not as young as I used to be."

"You're as young as you feel, Mrs. Renfru." And the woman did seriously look a decade younger than her years.

"Yes, well today I'm feeling ancient. I'm sorry to keep you in limbo, but as soon as I have this together, I'll let you know."

"Thank you, Mrs. Renfru. And make sure to take care of yourself." The situation might be messy, but that didn't change the fact that her landlady was a likeable old woman. "Worrying won't change anything."

"No dear, no it won't."

Lifting to her feet, Violet disconnected the call and slid the phone into her bag. She needed to follow her own advice. Worrying wasn't going to do anyone a bit of good. Planning, on the other hand, that was something her mother and father had drummed into her from the cradle. One of the many reasons she was able to have her own yoga studio at her age. Unfortunately, rewiring a building was not anywhere in those plans. Maybe she should ask her dad to help Mrs. Renfru. After all, what good was having banking connections if you didn't pull a few strings now and then? And though she'd promised herself she wasn't going to worry, she liked the idea of Mrs. Renfru fixing up the place a whole lot better than she liked the idea of a new landlord.

Violet pulled the glass door shut behind her and turned the lock. Her phone buzzed. Missed call from her grandmother. She let out a heavy sigh. What she needed now was a little of Lily's chocolate chip banana bread, Lucy's garlic shrimp, and her grandmother's smile. Not necessarily in that order. A bonfire on the beach with her cousins wouldn't hurt either, even if it was freezing outside.

Checking the time on her cell, Violet did some fast math. If she hurried home, by the time she showered and threw a few things into a bag, the height of rush hour would be over and she could make it to the lake by the first deal of the cards. The thought brought a smile to her face. She'd spent more weekends on the lake the past few months than she had in all of the last couple of years. Whatever changes this temporary setback brought, the bright side would be a plan that included more time at the lake. Yep, she could feel her Zen returning. Everything would work itself out. She was sure. She couldn't afford not to be.

CHAPTER TWO

Research was something Grant did well. He knew all about the Hart Land family legacy. In the family for generations, during the depression the property had been converted by a shrewd ancestor into rentals for the few fortunate society members who had not lost their shirts with the stock market crash and appreciated lakefront views.

Grant had seen magazine spreads, newspaper interviews, and enough aerial photos to know this particular property was A-plus prime. None of this understanding had done justice to the reality of his drive across Lawford Mountain. Rather than rush through after leaving the last construction site, he'd opted for a good night's sleep and switching to his personal car. Cruising along the curved roads under canopies of towering trees, he was doubly glad he'd decided to take the time out of his already overloaded schedule to make his pitch to the General in person.

Not that Grant didn't trust his grandfather's assessment of the prospects—he did. Pops was sharp as a box of tacks. Four years at the Naval Academy coupled with five years in the service had taught the older man everything he'd needed to know about discipline and honor and how to rise above the crowd for a Harvard MBA. From there, Garrett Whitaker climbed the corporate ladder up and out and into his own company. Built on a lengthy history of defense contracts, Pops sat on the board of directors of a very lucrative business.

A lead like Hart Land had been Grant's good fortune. Something that seemed to follow the Whitakers. A couple of weeks ago over dinner, his grandfather mentioned he'd heard from a checker playing buddy who owned a summer home on the mountain that the General had been more vocal of late about getting too old to be an innkeeper. By the end of the conversation Grant had agreed with his grandfather that if there was a time to strike a deal, now was it. Ever since, he'd been mentally planning a top-notch resort community with all the local amenities for the current generation of overly rich people eager for lakefront views—only this time, with a very luxurious touch. The dollar signs dancing a jig around the idea would make Joe very happy. The challenge—the General wouldn't return his calls.

If it turns out the man had no interest in selling and Grant couldn't find his price—after all, every man has his price—at least Grant would have a long weekend to catch up on the never ending mountains of paperwork.

Almost hidden behind oversized evergreens, what looked like a well-cared for original sign pointed the way to Hart Land. Taking the sharp right turn, Grant almost lost his breath when the magnificent old white three-story Victorian broke from between the trees. Perched at the top of the hill, the views from the approach were amazing. Oh yeah, definitely the coup of the decade. Already design possibilities on how to repurpose the grand old house were spinning in his head.

Rising from the landscape like a phoenix, a petite woman in a bright colored dress under a blood-red jacket stood among the white and yellow blooms. Sporting silver hair under a wide brim hat, a basket of fresh cut flowers dangled from one arm as she waved at him, clutching a pair of sheers in the other. The perfect reception for such a picturesque place. For an instant, Grant felt as though he might have been transported back in time to Rockwellian America.

"Welcome to Hart House." Having placed the sheers on the cut flowers, the statuesque woman extended her hand. "I'm Fiona Hart. You must be Mr. Whitaker. So pleased to have you."

Grant blinked, curious to know if there were so few guests or if the woman was merely that good an innkeeper. "The pleasure is all mine, and it's Grant."

"Very well, Grant. If you'll follow me into the main house, we'll get you checked in and then if you like, George will show you to your cabin."

"Thank you." He had no idea who George was, but had hoped that along with Fiona Hart, retired General Harold Hart might be here to greet him.

A young brunette in a colorful flowing skirt came bopping up the stairs and through the double wooden front doors.

"Oh good, Poppy." Fiona extended the basket. "Be a dear and

take these to Lucy.”

"Sure." She kissed Fiona on the cheek, shucked her jacket and set it aside. "Mom has to meet with Mrs. Bunker's family this morning. She's hoping Lucy has some extra cookies around."

"Oh, of course." The way Fiona Hart frowned, Grant wasn't sure which was the problem, the cookies, the mother, or the Bunker family. "Too bad we don't have any rum balls. Those would work better."

The brunette laughed. "I tried to tell Mom to break out the booze but that didn't go over very well."

"No. I would think not."

The younger woman turned to Grant and smiled.

"Oh, where are my manners. Grant," Fiona waved an arm, "this is Poppy, one of my granddaughters."

"Welcome." The woman smiled, then turned to her grandmother again. "I'd better hurry. Mom's running late."

"Now." Fiona glanced across the large entry. "Where were we?"

"Checking in," Grant said.

"Oh yes." The woman chuckled. "Of course. We're having unseasonably warm weather. If you enjoy hiking we've opened more trails around the property."

Walking the land would certainly help feed the well of possibilities. "Thank you. I'd like that."

He'd barely made it to the immense antique desk nestled to one corner of the warmly decorated entry when the weight of rapid footsteps sounded behind him. Laden with a pile of neatly folded towels, a tall blonde darted past him, shouting over her shoulder, "Lucy said to tell you these are the last of the new towels," and disappeared through a door under the winding staircase.

"That," Fiona smiled, "was my granddaughter Iris. She's here for a couple of days before leaving for India."

"India?"

"Yes, she was originally scheduled to leave for Thailand right after the holidays, but her boss had a business emergency of some sort and that trip was postponed. Now they're going to India. We see so little nowadays of some of our girls that it's nice to have them home for any reason."

Home. The word gave him pause. He knew from his research

that the General had nine granddaughters and more than half of them did not grow up on the lake. And yet, Fiona Hart had just referred to this place as home. Odds were if Mrs. Hart felt that way, so would her husband. Or would he? Didn't most military families claim they had no hometown? He'd have to keep that in mind. If he was about to talk a tired old man into selling his home, that would be a much different discussion than selling his business. And the more Grant saw of this property, the more he knew walking away from this deal was not an option.

"Fiona, dear." A man as tall as Grant's six foot plus frame came through the doors carrying a pile of chopped wood higher than anything Grant would have attempted in a single trip. "Forgive me traipsing through the house but Jim Frazier dropped this off in the front. What was that man thinking? Would never have happened under my command."

"Of course, dear. I'll be done here shortly and we can leave for your," her gaze drifted up to Grant and over to the man's departing back, "my trip to the yarn shop."

Despite Grant's instinct to reach forward and help, the General had mumbled an affirmative and continued through without a moment's hesitation, or time for Grant to react. What must have been a back door slammed shut hard enough for Grant to hear. Staring at the empty rear hall, he wondered if maybe his grandfather had been referring to some other tired and old general, because the man who had just whizzed past him looked anything but old or tired.

• • • •

Not since her last visit to the lake had Violet slept so late and so soundly. Going through her morning routine of stretches and breathing with the open window letting in all the fresh lakeside air went a long way toward restoring her peace of mind. Whether she liked to admit it or not, from the day the backed up flow of water from the leaky pipe finally burst through the sodden plaster walls and shut down her studio, she'd been teetering from concern to worry. Not terribly at first, but it hadn't taken long to know the blip on the radar could be a problem. Said and done.

At least the construction on her parents' cabin was complete, giving her a spacious and free place to stay. Her mom had outdone herself once again. Violet had to admit the old place where she and her sisters had spent a thousand summers growing up had morphed into a luscious retreat. With her mom's latest efforts, the wide open kitchen was simply to die for. Too bad Violet didn't plan on dying over a hot stove any time soon. She didn't mind tossing something together from time to time, especially if she wanted to avoid all the added sugar in prepackaged or restaurant foods, but cooking was not her favorite pastime. Not like Lucy the housekeeper, who was happiest in the kitchen, or her cousin Lily, the best baker known to man. Okay, maybe there was another baker as good somewhere else in the world but he or she was not known to Violet.

She'd barely made it around the corner of the cabin on the path to the main house when she spotted the sleek silver sports car parked in Hart House's front drive. "Wow." Anyone who rented vacation cabins from her grandfather was unlikely to be pinching pennies, but six figure automobiles weren't the norm either. "Wow."

"You're repeating yourself." Her cousin Cindy fell in step beside her.

"Wonder who drives it…"

"On my way to Mom's earlier, I spotted tall, dark and handsome talking to Grams."

"Are you sure he belongs to the car? It's been my experience that men who drive a car like that lean more toward the short, rotund and balding."

Cindy, short for Hyacinth, laughed. "Don't you think that's a bit of an exaggeration?"

"Maybe." But she wasn't committing.

"Oh look." Cindy shoved an elbow into Violet's side. "Here he comes."

The sight was impressive. Tall, dark and handsome definitely fit the bill. The other words that Cindy had failed to use were over-dressed and out of place. She could see the crease in his slacks from here, and if she wasn't mistaken, smell the leather in his shoes. Not that she had anything against leather accessories, but at the lake?

"Oh, my." Cindy's pace slowed. "Wonder if he's really alone."

"Impossible. No one who looks like that is ever alone." Rich and handsome. If they waited another minute, a buxom blonde was sure to come running out of the main house, no doubt dabbing her face or freshening her lipstick in a well practiced effort to put her Future Trophy Wives of America training to good use. Still. "Might be worth checking if he's married."

"Could it be Lucy is finally going to get it right?" Cindy hefted a bag at her hip. "I mean, if the reason she wants Sadie is to introduce me to Mr. Sports Car, I might be willing…"

Not till now had Violet realized Cindy had a pet carrier at her side. "Sadie?"

"The stray mama cat we rescued a while back. She's been our clinic kitty. Loves people, but lately she's been a bit out of sorts."

How does a person tell if a cat is out of sorts?

"Lucy suggested we stop by for a visit. See if the cat simply misses being free to roam."

"She is fixed, isn't she?" The last thing they needed were carbon copies of the orange tabby to roam around as well.

"Of course." Her steps slowed.

Violet shortened her pace to match. "What's wrong?"

"I was just thinking." Cindy looked to her cousin. "If Lucy *is* behind this, and she's asked me to bring the cat now to meet a new guest... something will inevitably go very wrong. Soon."

Cindy had a point. Lucy had a gift for a lot of things but matchmaking wasn't one of them. The fiasco with Lily and Danny Fleugel came to mind. And the fireplace smoke and the nearby firemen. "I don't know. Seems too contrived, even for Lucy."

"Oh, I hope so. I really would rather not find myself trapped with a con artist in a stolen car."

The way Lucy's track record ran, if she had indeed set this up, Cindy could have hit a bullseye with her worse case scenario. Though it would be a shame. The closer Violet got to the car, the sweeter looking the ride was, and now that she had a better view of the guy walking away from her grandmother, he looked rather delicious himself. Were those eyes that blue or was she imagining things? No ring. Could be interesting.

Mr. Sports Car turned in her direction and before he could catch her taking inventory, Violet shifted her attention to the car. The leather seats seemed to be inviting her to take a load off and see the world with the wind in her face. Daring to run her hands along the seams, she couldn't help but think of all the things that the price of this remarkable automobile could pay for: feed the hungry, educate the poor. Heck, maybe even help with the mess Brandon Carter left the mountain.

"Violet," Cindy muttered through clenched teeth.

Before she could see what her cousin wanted, Violet retreated a step into something hard, throwing her off balance. Her arms went up, and the next thing she knew, two vises enclosed around her arms.

"I have the same reaction," the deep, rolling voice washed over her.

This close and personal, she was positive the eyes were blue. Very blue. Deeper than his voice blue. *Speak, Violet. Speak.* "Uh." *Brain freeze.* "What was that?"

The smile that framed perfectly straight white teeth slipped. "The car. I have the same reaction to her. First time I saw her, I couldn't resist taking her home." Slowly loosening his grip, he eased back a step.

"Her?" Not the most intelligible thing Violet had ever said, but the single syllable beat *uh*. Besides, she was enormously thankful he hadn't made more of a fuss of her tripping over... what had she tripped over? Heaven help her. One good looking guy in sight and she was turning into her cousin Lily.

"The car is too pretty to be a man." That toothpaste commercial smile was back and for just a second, Violet thought she might tip over again.

"A little chauvinistic, don't you think?" Cindy patted the soft-sided case resting against her hip.

So entranced by Mr. Sports Car, Violet had actually forgotten her cousin was at her side.

"My apologies." That smile actually grew wider, and his arm gestured toward the carrier. "Would you like some help with that?"

Cindy's left brow raised up high as her chin dipped. A do-I-look-that-helpless glare spoke volumes.

Mr. Gorgeous swallowed a chuckle. "I'll take that as a no."

Smart man. Good powers of observation too. Most of the men Violet knew would not have caught on to Cindy's silent communication.

"Are you two going to stand out here all day? Grams says to leave our new guest alone. He's here to rest." Hands on her hip, Iris stood, shaking her head and rolling her eyes skyward. Clearly repeating the words for their grandmother's benefit and didn't believe the man was here to rest any more than Violet or Cindy did.

"Sorry." Cindy smiled politely at the new guest, skirting around him.

"Enjoy your stay." Violet hurried around the opposite side. She couldn't be completely sure, but she could have sworn if she turned around, she'd see the man staring after her. Now she was out of character, clumsy and delusional. What was wrong with her?

CHAPTER THREE

From inside Hart House, Violet could hear the roar of the sleek car come to life. Sounded more like it held lions under the hood instead of horsepower. "Do we know anything about Mario Andretti?"

"Who?" Lucy looked up from drying her hands by the sink.

Cindy set the carrier down on the island counter. "The guy with the sports car."

"Well, why didn't you jut say so?" Lucy waved a thumb over her shoulder at their grandmother already seated at her favorite winter spot in the tiny solarium off the kitchen. "Your grandmother checked him in. I haven't seen him yet."

"But you know who he is?" Cindy pushed.

Lucy shrugged and waved her finger at the cat carrier. "Not really. He only made the reservation a few days ago. Didn't say much. Though your grandmother mentioned he drives a snazzy car."

That was definitely one word for the convertible.

"Shall we take this gal to see Ms. Fiona?" Not waiting for a reply, Lucy took the pet carrier from Cindy, slung it onto her shoulder and led the three cousins across the kitchen.

Iris was the first to veer out of line to her grandmother's side, each granddaughter giving her a quick kiss on the cheek before taking a seat at the round table.

For as long as Violet could remember, her grandmother had been a patron of the arts. Monthly luncheons at the women's art league was a favorite thing for her. Parties for sculptors and painters to rival the soirees her mom threw in Boston were famous in Lawford. It was obvious where her mom had learned to be the hostess with the mostess. A Lawford by birth, Gram's family had once owned most of this mountain and probably still owned most of the granite. "What exactly are we doing now?"

"Waiting for your grandfather. We're going to my specialty yarn shop today."

"You like that place, don't you?" Violet asked. At least once a month her grandfather took Grams on the long drive almost to Boston for yarn.

"Indeed, I do." Grams smiled.

"So what's the plan till you leave?" Cindy asked.

"Hooking, dear." The sweet woman, whose classic features made her an excellent candidate for any beauty product advertisement, grinned merrily.

Iris was the one to flinch. "Say again?"

"I've joined a hooking club."

Cindy blinked and Violet laughed. There had to be something here but for the life of her Violet couldn't figure out what her grandmother was talking about. To this day, what Violet couldn't be sure of was if the woman said things like that just to get a rise out of her family or if she was actually that naive. Somehow Violet doubted it was the latter.

Since the opening of the Olla Podrida arts village, Grams had gone from one artsy craft to another. Violet had seen the older woman do her best—and worst—at macramé, tatting, knitting, and most recently crocheting. This simply had to be her next effort. Especially with spools of yarn piled all around her, which Violet doubted were for the cat. And odds were whatever she was up to had absolutely nothing to do with the way it sort of sounded.

"I don't suppose you'd like to clarify that?" Iris shifted in the seat beside her grandmother.

Pulling a pair of scissors from her nearby craft bag, Grams smiled up at Iris. "Clarify hooking rugs?"

"Ah." Iris sat back. "Of course."

Violet grinned at her cousin. "What else could it be?"

Iris shot Violet a withering glare, one that she was well practiced at as a professional nanny for the rich and spoiled, before turning to Lucy. "So do we have a plan for Red there?"

From the partially unzipped carrier, the kitty's orange head stuck out, eyeing her surroundings.

"Not sure yet." Lucy stood back watching.

Grams set the yarn she'd been wrapping around a small circular piece of cardboard aside. "Sadie, dear, did you miss us?"

As though the animal had been waiting for instruction, she squirmed her body up and out through the small opening and sashayed across the table to the older woman.

"I thought she was feral?" Violet asked, watching how the kitty sidled up to Grams, rubbing against her hands and purring.

Cindy shook her head. "Once we caught her she was skittish but friendly with folks she recognized. My guess is she had some human contact before she settled in under the porch here. But this," she waved at Sadie now curled up in Grams' lap, "this is something new."

Propping her chin on Grams' arm, the cat stretched her back legs out and closed her eyes.

"I have one question." Cindy looked from the cat to Lucy. "If Grams has such a way with her, why did it take so long to catch her?"

"Because," her grandmother smiled, "Sadie isn't fond of Lady or Sarge. As soon as your grandfather took them for a ride to visit with his friend Cam so the dogs could play together, she came right out to visit us. Even introduced us to her kitties."

"No," Lucy shook her head, "she introduced *you* to her kitties. Me she scratched."

Grams looked down at the now sleeping kitty. "Momentary misunderstanding."

Yeah, that was Violet's grandmother. Always looking to the bright side. If someone asked her to explain the origins of the Civil War, she'd probably say it was a momentary misunderstanding between the North and South.

"So, Grams," Cindy moved the carrier to the floor and took a seat, "looks like you've got a cat."

"I don't know about that. I think she'd be happier in a canine free environment."

Cindy shook her head and grinned. "Like it or not Grams, that is your cat. Lady and Sarge are simply going to have to learn to live with her."

Grams continued to pet the snoozing feline. "Well, I suppose if she stays out of my yarn, we might be able to work something out."

"Agreed," Violet echoed, still not knowing anything more about Mario Andretti than she had a few minutes ago, and she was curious.

Very curious. The man seemed so terribly out of place. The car, the clothes, the city boy air, none of it fit with the rustic charm of Hart House on Lake Lawford. Not that any of it mattered. She had more important things to be filling her mind. Like what to do about her studio. After yesterday's yoga session, she'd briefly glanced at the real estate section of the online paper before deciding the only chance of saving her inner peace would be to continue her search here, where even if she wasn't totally at peace, at least her surroundings were.

"Iris, dear." Lucy smiled and even though she was addressing Violet's cousin, that familiar twinkle in her eye and lilt in her voice set off Violet's early matchmaking radar. "The gentleman in the Elm will be needing some of those new towels you sorted for us earlier."

"Oh no." Iris shook her head. "I came to report for Sunday dinner one last time before this next long trip. Did my duty. I've stayed as long as I can. Now I *have* to head home. Helping men in Maseratis is not part of my job description."

"It's a Lamborghini," Lucy corrected.

"Is it?" Violet's inner warning system for whenever Lucy was up to something was now blaring loudly in her head. "I thought you didn't know much about the new visitor?"

"Oh, well," Lucy looked about the room as though searching for a hole to hide in, "I may have overheard a little."

"A little?" Cindy repeated.

"Our Mr. Whitaker?" Grams looked up from the attention she'd been paying the snoozing kitty.

"If he belongs to the sports car, that would be the one," Violet said.

"Nothing special." Grams left the kitty snoozing on her lap and began snipping the edges of the yarn disc. "Just another guest here for some rest and relaxation and a little hiking."

Violet's gaze drifted in the direction of the lower cabins, imagining the car parked in front of the Elm. If Mr. Italian leather shoes was here to hike, any day now she'd be taking over as commandant of the Marine Corps.

• • • •

With a carryon bag, Grant didn't have much to unpack. In only a few minutes he'd hung up his slacks and shirts, opened every cabinet and closet, tested the bed, and turned the television on then off. The cabins were simple. Homey. Adequate. He couldn't remember ever vacationing anywhere in his entire life that didn't offer cable television, internet access and room service. Not even summer camp had felt quite this…isolated. And yet, the view from every single expansive window gave him pause. What would it be like to work every day with filtered views to the lake rather than a picture frame of the office building across the street? Not that he spent much time looking out windows.

With only a few days cleared in his schedule, he needed to work quickly. Fiona Hart was right about one thing: the sunny day beckoned for a nice walk. Get the lay of the land. Fine tune the ideas bouncing around in his head and with any luck, bump into the innkeeper himself and make an offer he couldn't resist. Perhaps a walk around the main house and where the firewood was stored would be a good start. If he didn't run into the General along his path, at least he was assured a seat at the family table tonight. With fewer restaurants open this time of year, Mrs. Hart had been gracious enough to extend a dinner invitation.

Grabbing his coat from a nearby hook, Grant pulled the door closed behind him and locked it by sliding the key with the bright blue pom-pom into the knob. Something about the old fashioned key and lock made him smile. If a guest's wish was to go back in time fifty years to the days of party lines, back doors without locks, and three network television channels, this place probably seemed like heaven.

Looking up the hill toward Hart House, he quickly decided searching out the General could wait. Anticipation of seeing the waterfront views far exceeded his eagerness to meet the retired Marine and cut a deal. Considering how eager he was to do just that, anticipation was running off the charts. He'd not had time to study elevation charts and county plat books, but a stroll down hill and along the shore would go a long way to feeding his final plans.

Following the gravel path leading in the opposite direction to the lake, he began a mental list of changes. Too many trees crowded the property. Some would have to be cut down. A shame really. Even with his best efforts to preserve the ambiance, it simply had to be done. The money is in the view. On top of that the roots made for uneven ground. The new development would require paved walkways. Or better yet, pave stones. Something to mimic nature but completely level for older, wealthier buyers and vacationers. Yes. The picture was coming more clearly to mind. When the trees broke and the view opened wide, the hairs on the nape of his neck actually stood on end. Picture perfect. Another few feet and he could see the beachfront. Another selling point. The picture was getting better and better with every step. Another zero slid easily onto the end of the dollar amounts dancing in his head.

The smell of burning wood caught his attention. At first he thought it was a wild fire. With all these trees and dead wood lying about, it wouldn't take but a single careless spark to destroy the wonderful vista. A second whiff and scan of the horizon and he realized the smell came from a small intentional fire down the beach.

Too far to make out who, he could see a single figure seated on the ground, poking at the burning wood, sending spurts of flames up as oxygen fueled the fire. Instinct had his mouth fall open, ready to holler at the fool for playing around with flames and then the practiced moves, the fearless approach of the person watching the dancing flames had his mouth snapping shut. He reminded himself he was the urban interloper in this pristine setting, not the figure ahead who seemed to be almost one with the fire. So much so that his pace slowed until he inched to a stop.

"Are you going to stand there all day?" the decidedly female voice called to him without looking up.

"I was thinking about it."

A face he recognized turned in his direction, a lazy smile slowly lifting the corners of her mouth. "Well, let me know what you decide."

"I'm thinking," he moved closer, "it's a little cold for sitting on the beach."

The woman who not too long ago had admired his wheels shook her head, chuckling. "Seems the chilly day is the perfect excuse for a beach bonfire."

"Is that what this is?" He stood close enough to see she sat on a large wool blanket. "Room for one more?"

Without saying a word, she waved a hand toward the empty space beside her.

"Thanks. We weren't properly introduced before." He stuck his hand out. "Grant Whitaker."

The lovely brunette accepted his hand. "Violet Preston. Nice to meet you."

"The pleasure's all mine, and you're right."

"Usually am." She tipped her head in his direction again and smiled more brightly. "Sorry, couldn't resist. What about?"

"The fire is just perfect on a crisp, cool day like this."

"If I'd known I would have company I'd have brought marshmallows. Then it would be truly perfect."

He looked at the expansive water views in front of him. Somehow, this low to the ground, the vista seemed even more… magical. "Looks pretty perfect to me."

"True." She poked at the fire again, sending another flash of flame up the center.

"You're pretty good at this."

She muffled a laugh. "I've been around bonfires since before I could walk. Everyone around here knows how to start one and how to stoke one. I'd probably be drummed out of the family if I couldn't start a decent fire."

"I see." Living in cold winter country, he and every other male in the state knew how to stack and build a fire, but that didn't mean he actually put that knowledge into practice. In his pocket the phone buzzed. Not till now had he realized it hadn't sounded since crossing into this Rockwellian world. To his surprise, he had at least a dozen texts.

"Best cell phone reception is in the middle of the lake, but the shoreline is pretty decent too." She kept an eye on him as his fingers flew over the screen, responding quickly and concisely to each message. "You're frowning."

Of course he was. If the only place his cell phone would receive messages and calls was on the shoreline, he might be sleeping out here the next couple of days.

"You know," she said as he paused to read two new responses, "the idea of Hart Land is to unplug."

"Yes, well, that's not going to happen."

Her brows rose high on her forehead.

It dawned on him that revealing he was only here for business might not be well received. He also quickly determined that the use of his phone to remain plugged in was not well received by the lovely brunette sharing her blanket and fire with him. Completely convinced he wanted this deal now more than ever, and still unsure of the situation or how best to accomplish his goals, ticking off a granddaughter was not in his best interest. Ignoring another response, he dropped his phone back into his breast pocket. "On the other hand, I thought a nice long walk around the property would be fun."

Her gaze washed quickly over him and came to a stop at his feet. "Not dressed like that."

"What's wrong with how I'm dressed?"

"Nothing if you're spending an afternoon at the country club, but those nice crisp khakis aren't meant for a stroll through the woods. Or the shoes."

"The shoes?" He looked down at his feet. They were his most comfortable loafers.

"For one thing, they're leather soles. I'm amazed you made it this far without falling on your rear. And I'm pretty sure there isn't an Italian shoe made that's meant to be worn in the sand, never mind near the water."

She did have a point. Already he had a spot on his pant leg from where he'd bumped into the mossy side of a tree. And his shoes... "How did you know they were Italian?"

"Lucky guess." She grinned widely and he got the feeling luck had nothing to do with her assessment.

"You might want to change before you venture any further." Again, she poked at the burning wood pile.

Though he did have steel tipped boots for the construction sites, it hadn't occurred to him to bring anything other than casual dress clothes. Casual for him. At least he'd left his suits at home. "I didn't bring anything different."

Those sleek brows shot up again. "All you brought were loafers and pressed pants?"

He nodded. "I could probably pop into town and pick something up."

"You could." Dropping the stick she'd used as a poker and brushing her hands together, she nodded. "You'll find most of what you need on Main Street."

"Any place in particular?"

"Start at the hardware store. They have lots of affordable jeans." Shaking her head, she pushed to her feet. "And you might want to ask the General to lend you a vehicle. That car is going to bring out summer pricing."

"Jeans are more in the summer?"

"Tourist season." She smiled. "I think it's in the constitution somewhere that towns that earn eighty percent of their income thirty percent of the year get to charge more during that thirty percent."

"Got it. I don't suppose you'd consider giving me a lift into town?" The words had slipped out of his mouth before he'd given them any thought, but now that they were hanging out there, he realized it might have been the best idea he'd had all day.

CHAPTER FOUR

When she'd found out that her landlady was pulling the rug out from under her world as she knew it, her plans for the next few days consisted of crawling into the modern internet world and hunting for a new place of business. And to her chagrin, maybe even a new apartment to go with it. What she did not anticipate was walking down Main Street beside Mr. Tall Dark and Handsome.

"Floyd's?" Grant's steps slowed, his gaze lingering on the activity inside.

"Floyd is the one cutting the customer's hair. The two playing checkers and chatting away are Ralph, a family neighbor, and Ned Baker, another friend. Both the General's cohorts."

"Interesting," he muttered.

"Some days I do feel like I've stepped back in time." She pointed across the street to Henry's Hardware. "That's what we need."

"You were serious?" Grant's feet seemed to be rooted to the cement. "You want me to buy jeans at the hardware store?"

"If you want we can go up the street a bit to Mac's Menswear but you're going to pay a lot more for jeans that I'm guessing," her gaze dropped to his Italian loafers, "you won't ever wear again."

"I wear jeans." His chin lifted with a hint of defiance.

"Really?" Now the question was whether to pin him down or let it ride. No, her blood pressure didn't need to take this battle on. "Fine. We'll go to Mac's."

"Thank you." He followed her up the sidewalk.

"Who am I to stop you from throwing away your money." Not that it mattered. Judging from the car the guy drove he probably lit candles for romantic dinners with hundred dollar bills.

Grant came to a dead stop. His eyes met hers and for the life of her she couldn't determine what exactly he was searching for, but she could feel the intensity of his gaze clear down to her toes. "Let's take a look at Henry's."

Blue. Unchanged since their earlier encounter, his eyes were a crystal blue, the color of a summer sky on a clear day, and they continued to hold her undivided attention. Unable to find words, she merely nodded and found herself struggling to take a step back. The power to silently mesmerize a person with a single look probably got this guy anything he wanted. Literally shaking her head, she broke the connection and stepped aside. "This way."

"Yes, ma'am." He smiled and crossed the street at her side.

The overhead bell rang as the heavy glass door encased in weathered oak swung open.

"Be right with you," a voice called from somewhere in the distance.

"This way." Violet moved down the center of the large store past the hammers, electrical, and nail aisle to turn at the work clothes. The store hadn't changed in all the years she'd summered at the lake. Not a nail or screw had been moved. As expected, the jeans were nestled along with the painter's pants and overalls. "What's your size?"

"Thirty-four, thirty-four."

Running her finger along the shelf labels, Violet resisted the urge to turn around and check out the man's size for herself. She and her cousin had determined tall from a distance earlier in the day, a thirty-four inseam would certainly confirm that. "Here we go."

Still not looking behind her, she handed off the pants and marched up the aisle.

"Now what?" Grant fell in step behind her. He was pretty good about following her. Most men she'd known wouldn't move an inch without her first laying out a detailed flight plan.

"Shoes."

"Here?" Incredulity rang clear in his voice.

"Maybe."

"Maybe?" Poor guy looked totally befuddled.

"Not sure." Making the man wear steel tipped shoes might be overkill for a hike up the hill.

The overhead bell dinged again and Louise Franklin came waddling over. "I thought that was you I saw rushing across the street."

"Hello, Ms. Franklin." Violet plastered on the brightest smile she could muster. Louise, who'd worked at the pharmacy since before the beginning of time could be counted on to keep her finger on the pulse of Lawford and its residents. And in this case, visitors.

Louise casually took Grant in from his over six foot high head to his leather clad feet. If the woman hadn't lost her touch, she had probably already calculated the value of his wardrobe—and possibly his net worth—to the penny. Without a doubt, Violet and Grant were about to become the latest town fodder.

"This is the latest guest at Hart Land." Violet waved between the two people standing on either side of her. "Grant Whitaker. Louise Franklin has worked at the pharmacy for—"

"Since the dawn of time," Louise interrupted. "It's a pleasure to meet you. And what may I ask brings you to our hardware store?"

"Louise." Tom, the assistant manager, came out from the back. "Sorry for the delay. Signing off on a large shipment and needed to get it sorted. I have that bird seed you wanted."

Louise Franklin's eyes doubled in size before a stiff smile quickly hid her momentary surprise. "Oh, yes. I'd almost forgotten."

"Isn't that why you're here?" Poor Tom. The former Marine was a really nice guy but clearly didn't have a clue that Louise lived for fresh gossip and spotting Violet walking in town with a stranger trumped bird seed any day of the week.

Louise straightened her shoulders and tightened her grip on her handbag strap. "Yes, of course. It's so much more affordable to get the fifty pound bag of seed here than those little bags at the pet store."

"Where are you parked?"

Louise blinked. Violet was pretty sure the woman didn't want to move along without having acquired at least some new information for the grapevine, but heaving out a resigned sigh, she threw her thumb over her shoulder. "Across the street. I can pull up in back if you'd like."

"Perfect. I'll meet you by the loading dock."

Louise nodded and with a hesitant smile, waved at Violet. "Tell your grandparents I send my hellos."

"Will do." Violet waved back.

"So," Tom turned to face her, "finding everything you need?"

Pointing at the pants Grant held out in front of him, Violet faced Tom. "Is there someplace to try these on?"

"All we've got is the bathroom."

"I don't know if that will be necessary," Grant spoke up.

"No problem." Tom took a step back. "I'll take care of Louise Franklin while you try those on, then I'll be right back."

"Sounds good." Violet grabbed a pair of lighter prewashed jeans and added it to Grant's pile. "Might as well try these too. See which one strikes your fancy."

Grant's brow rose up on his forehead.

Yeah, even she recognized jeans and fancy didn't belong in the same sentence. Especially not when said jeans were about to be worn by the wealthy Mr. Tall Dark and Handsome.

• • • •

How did he politely explain that the benefit of men's pants being sized by waist and inseam meant there was little need to try on things? In less than five seconds he concluded, much like opting to shop for pants here the way Violet had suggested, instead of at the men's store he might have preferred, some things simply fell into a self-preservation policy of *it's easier to do as the lady asks than try to make sense of it.* "I'll be right back."

Almost at the bathroom door near the rear offices, Grant crossed paths with another man. Did everyone in this town smile all the time?

"Finding everything you need?"

"Yes. Just looking for the men's room to try these on."

"There you go." The gentleman pointed.

"Thanks." Inside the bare-bones restroom, Grant took a moment to answer a few ignored texts and quickly was in and out of the two jeans. As he'd anticipated, they fit like the proverbial glove. While he leaned toward the darker, more pristine looking pair, the lighter ones looked more lived in and for his mission of leaving Lake Lawford with a contract to buy in hand, comfortable and lived-in was probably the way to go.

"Violet, when did you get in town?"

Grant opened the door in time to hear the second gentleman from a few minutes ago address his customer. Grant had heard about small towns before, but was beginning to think that old cliché about everyone knowing everyone held a lot more truth than he'd expected. Walking toward the voices, Violet embracing the man came into view. The bright smile on her face as she pulled back told him she might know this Lawford citizen better than most. And why did that idea make him want to growl at the guy?

"You're looking as relaxed as ever." The man smiled.

Relaxed? What the heck kind of compliment is that? Grant maneuvered around the man's back and positioned himself at Violet's side, replacing the urge to snarl with a practiced smile. He had no business interrupting and didn't care. His cell hummed from a text response; whoever it was could wait.

Not bad looking and in pretty good shape, the guy's gaze darted from Violet to Grant, did a fast survey of his potential competition, and then returned to Violet. Not that Grant had a horse in this race, but they were both men and knew how the game was played. "He's with you?"

"New guest at the lake." Violet rolled a lazy shoulder, momentarily gesturing with her chin towards his shoes. "Needs more appropriate attire for a…uh… stroll in the woods."

"I see." He nodded and shot his hand out. "Jake Harper."

"My sister's fiancé," Violet explained.

It took Grant all of three seconds to determine by the way the guy's face lit up at the label that his posturing over Violet was that of protective big brother-to-be, not a contender. "Grant Whitaker. Nice to meet you."

"Whitaker?" Jake narrowed his gaze and cocked his head to one side. "It's a long shot, but by any chance do you have any relatives in the Navy?"

Odd question, but then again, anyone who read the financial sections of the paper would recognize the name. "Yes."

Jake's brows rose. Wrong answer? Or perhaps too short a response?

This wasn't a corporate board meeting. They weren't fighting over a property. Grant had to remind himself he was in small town USA. "My grandfather served a few years after attending the Naval

Academy."

Jake's face lit up. "I'll be. Garret?"

Cautiously, Grant nodded.

"Talk about a small world. My grandfather was a Commander in the Navy before he retired. He loves telling stories about his days at Annapolis. And there are a lot of stories about Garret Whitaker. Wait till I tell him I ran into his grandson."

"That is a small world. I'll be honest, when Pops gets into reminiscing mode, he tosses around a lot of names. I couldn't say if I'd remember any one of them." His phone buzzed again and this time he opted for a quick response.

"Of course." The front bell rang and Jake looked up. "I'd better get back to work. Let me know if you guys need anything else."

"Thanks, and I'll tell Pops I ran into you. What was your grandfather's name?"

"Eugene Harper."

A vague memory tickled the back of Grant's mind, and then it hit. "Eugene as in, is that *you* gene?"

"Yep. That would be him." Jake grinned and took a step back. "I really do have to run. Nice meeting you."

Grant smiled back as the man turned and hurried across the store.

"Even for Lawford, that's a small world." Violet shook her head and twisted to face him. "Did they fit?"

"Yep. I'm going to take these." He held up the lighter pants.

Violet's eyes widened showing their surprise. "Really? I would have bet you'd go for the darker jeans."

And technically she would have been right, but she didn't have all the facts yet. Of course, if she did know he was here to buy and transform the sleepy family land into a premiere—and very plugged-in—luxury destination, instead of helping him shop for more appropriate clothing, she might have merely tossed him into the lake.

CHAPTER FIVE

O kay, this is some seriously delicious ice cream." When Violet had suggested a post-shopping ice cream break, he thought the woman was nuts. After all, he wasn't five years old and most people would consider this time of year too cold for ice cream. Now he wished he'd ordered something larger than a single scoop.

"Told ya." Violet took another spoonful of her butter pecan and flashed a cheeky grin. "Have I ever lied to you?"

"No," he swallowed a chuckle and cleared his throat, "can't say that you have."

"See." Grinning, she waved a spoon at him before digging in for another scoopful.

"Actually, it never occurred to me that you weren't telling the truth, I just never thought I'd find ice cream this good in such a small town." Or enjoy eating it seated rather than on the move in his car. His phone buzzed and between bites he took a minute to tap a response, eager to return to his afternoon snack.

She gazed up over the rim of her double scoop cup. "Maybe it's this good because it *is* a small town."

Contemplating trying another flavor, Grant scraped up the last spoonful of the best vanilla bean ice cream he'd ever had. "I'm not sure I get the logic of that one."

"Not only homemade, but local cream from local grass-fed cows. That sort of thing. Millie owns this place. It's been in the family for generations and like her ancestors, she still makes the ice cream the old-fashioned way."

So far, his introduction to Lawford had shown him old-fashioned was more than a convenient adjective. From the barber pole outside Floyd's, to the throwback hairdryers visible through the window of Betty's Cut n Set, to just about every person being on a first name basis, old-fashioned was the standard around here. "You really love it here, don't you?"

Violet nodded. "Yeah, I suppose I do."

"Most people raised in small towns like this are desperate to get out."

"Ah." She smiled. "But you see, I wasn't technically raised here."

"Technically?"

"Boston born and bred. Summered here at the lake, every summer, without fail, until college. There's nothing like communing with Mother Nature to shake off the Zen-stealing stress of city life, and there's no place in the world better to do that than here at the lake." Her face lit up like a small child describing their first bicycle on Christmas morning.

"And then?" Slowly, the picture of what Mrs. Hart had described as *home* was becoming much clearer, and his job description was growing in complexity. Definitely not the easy pickings his grandfather had implied.

"Life." She shrugged. "Sometimes I'd only make it up to the lake for a few weeks. Some times only weekends. Over time it's gotten harder and harder to earn a living and visit the lake."

And wasn't that the truth. Earning a living seemed a misnomer. The more a person worked, the less likely there would be time left over for living. Maybe when this deal was done he could schedule a real vacation. He was rather fond of Paris.

"So." She set her empty cup down and settled back in the iron chair. "Why are you here now?"

He considered his options. How truthful did he need to be at this stage of what he hoped would become negotiations? After all, he hadn't even spoken to the General yet. Heck, he hadn't even met the General yet. Carefully choosing his words was a talent that had come in handy more than once. Being honest didn't mean a person had to always reveal everything he knew right up front, but somehow he felt today more than ever it mattered. "I'm here at the suggestion of my grandfather."

"The one that used to be in the Navy?"

He nodded. "The one and only."

"So it was Granddad who thought you needed to get away from the real world?"

Chuckling, he set his empty ice cream container on the table. Time for more of that honesty thing. "Far from it. He sent me out this way to scout potential property for a land deal."

Her brow dipped between her eyes. "Real estate?"

Now he really wished he had more ice cream to munch on and stall. "Yes."

"What kind of real estate?"

"Mostly commercial—"

"Commercial?" She cut him off. "Around here?"

"What's wrong with around here?"

She came forward, leaning on her elbows, and met his eyes without hesitation. "Well for one thing, none of the small towns on this mountain need a shopping mall."

The last thing he wanted to put in around here was a shopping mall. "Then there's nothing to worry about. I was thinking more along the lines of living space." With a shop or restaurant, but he'd save that for later.

The creases between her brow deepened. "You want to build condos?"

It wasn't a question. If anything, it came out more like an accusation. "Possibly." That was the truth. He had been thinking more of a resort, but maybe a little of both would be good. Right now he still didn't know for sure where the General stood on his family land, and the whole reason for the outing this afternoon was so that he'd be better prepared to investigate the surroundings and determine the best use for Hart Land. And the most convincing offer. The continued intensity of her gaze suggested now would be a good time to change the subject. "What about you? What do you do when you're not here visiting the family?"

"I teach yoga."

Okay, that was unexpected. Not that he had any idea what he expected, only that yoga wasn't it. *Weren't yoga people flakey airheads?* Then again, she did seem to seek out communion with trees.

The frown creasing her forehead gave way to a muffled laugh. "Don't look so surprised."

He shook away the vision of a nineteen sixties flower child

sitting in a lotus position. Quickly his mind ran the numbers. Making money—preferably lots of money—was a basic requirement for running a business. He should know, his family had perfected the art of doing both. "Forgive me. Business must be good if you can spend more time now at the lake."

"I wish." She rolled her eyes. "I live in a very old building. Lately some of its systems have been showing their age. Since my studio is in the same building, whenever something goes wrong that isn't an easy fix, I get to come hang out on the lake."

"So it's not all bad?"

"Not once in a while, but lately I'm starting to feel like the whole building is getting ready to collapse around me. Last couple of times it was the heater. This time it's a broken water pipe."

Grant sucked in a hiss. Nothing worse than water leaks and old buildings. And for the umpteenth time since striking cell phone range in town, his phone buzzed. A quick peek at the number told him the caller could wait. Setting it down on the table, he looked up and noticed some of the sunshine in her expression had dimmed. She didn't need him telling her the pitfalls of older buildings. "Hopefully as soon as it's all cleaned up, everything should be good as new. Maybe even better."

"From your mouth to God's ears. Assuming I can still afford it."

He sneaked another peek at his phone again. "Excuse me?"

"Nothing. Never mind." She stood. "We should head back to the house. Dusk still comes early. And now that you have a decent pair of pants and sturdy hiking shoes, you can beat out the sunset."

She was right. He had a job to do and not a lot of time to do it in. Normally he would have been the one nagging her to hurry up and wait. But this time he was enjoying the company even more than the ice cream. He actually wished there was another reason to linger in town. In their brief stroll, he'd learned about Jake, the hardware store owner, and his whirlwind romance with her sister, the heart surgeon. About Betty and the divine intervention to purchase a beauty parlor already christened with her name, and of course, how Floyd the Barber wasn't really Floyd at all. Violet had even thrown in an abridged—so she claimed—version of her cousin Lily's up-and-coming bakery, and wedding, not necessarily in that order. This town put the Q in quaint, and the company was exceptional. "Sounds like a plan. And thank you again for escorting me around, helping with the new things I wanted."

Lifting her hand to her mouth, she made a valiant effort to hide her laugh. "I don't know about that *wanted* part."

Since he had not said a single argumentative word about the shopping expedition and yet she'd picked up on his earlier indifference, he could only assume Miss Yoga Instructor had both a memory for detail and very good instincts. "You made an excellent argument for my not having any business wandering through the woods in my favorite loafers and khaki colored pants. Even if they're a darker khaki." Though quite frankly, he probably did not have near as much walking planned as his escort for the day must have assumed.

She made her way to the door. Based on their interaction with every other friend and neighbor they'd bumped into this afternoon, the goodbye conversation with Millie the owner only took a fraction of the time he had expected it to. Considering the small size of this town, and that through the years she'd only lived here part time—if that much—they'd bumped into an awful lot of people that she not only knew and knew well, but who knew her and every member of her Boston family and their current, though distant, happenings.

Looking down the short street, he really did wish he had more time to spend in town. Not only exploring the community, but exploring it with one very lovely yoga teacher.

• • • •

What was that saying, *Life is what happens while you're busy making other plans?* The last couple of days definitely counted as life happening. Violet had managed to spend all of ten minutes on the beach, stoking the fire, and perusing her phone for a new permanent locale for her studio. That's when another saying popped into her head, *It takes money to make money.* In those few minutes before Grant strolled into her line of sight, she'd quickly decided wallowing in a tad of self-pity might be in order.

"I lost you."

Blinking, Violet turned her gaze from a distant point down Main

Street to the man who had come to a stop a step behind her.

"You haven't said a word since we left the Village Creamery and now you just walked past your car."

Sure enough, Grant stood by her compact SUV. "I guess my mind wandered."

"If that frown is any indication, not someplace pretty."

"No." She clicked the key fob. "My building."

"And the leaky pipes." He opened the driver's side door for her before trotting back to the passenger side.

"And the pipes. And the mold. And the electrical. And the new owners."

"That's a lot of ands. Maybe you should start from the beginning."

Turning the key in the ignition, she glanced out the windows and thought, what the hell. Didn't strangers make the best therapists? "A few years ago, I truly stumbled into a sweet deal."

Grant nodded and she pulled out of the parking spot, pointing the car toward Hart Land.

"I'd been living in a nice little one bedroom apartment in this charming older building."

"Lipstick on a pig," he mumbled.

"Excuse me?"

Grant chuckled. "From the long list of things going wrong you've mentioned before and now, I'd say what you call charming is what we in the business of renovation call—"

"Lipstick on a pig. Got it. Anyhow, I hadn't been in the building long when a retail space on the first floor put up a going out of business sign. A little dress shop that had probably been in the building since before I was born."

"What makes you say that?"

"Maybe because Lillian's isn't a chain store and, according to the store manager, *the* Lillian had retired a decade before, only popping in to visit a few times a year. Once she passed away, her children felt no obligation to keep the place open. Timing is everything."

"Isn't it always?" He smiled. A nice bright smile that went a long way to making her glad she was telling him her troubles.

"While chatting with the manager about the sign the building owner came in. It was the first time I'd met Mrs. Renfru. Turns out she's a super sweet older lady who was not at all looking forward to having a vacant space."

"Few landlords are."

"No, I suppose not. Anyhow, the place wasn't overly huge but not too small either. It had a good size private bathroom and a few dressing rooms, and a small office that opened to a little employee lunchroom type thing. The best part, though, was the wood floors. Real hardwood floors throughout, even in the lunchroom and office."

"If it's as old as you say, back in those days, oak flooring was cheap. Some builders used oak planks for subfloor."

"Oh well, that would certainly explain it. As I admired the floors and mentioned how great they'd be for a yoga studio, Mrs. Renfru lit up. Next thing I knew I had a studio at the same rent Lillian had been paying. Mrs. Renfru was more than eager to turn the place over at a bargain if it meant no loss of income due to a quick turnaround."

"That is rather unusual. Most landlords are all about the bottom line."

"Not Mrs. Renfru. I think this is the only building she owns, and I think she counted heavily on the monthly income."

Grant nodded. Politely not pointing out to her that she'd just stated the obvious for any landlord.

"It's been a win win for everyone since," she added.

"And now?"

"The leaks have uncovered new problems and Mrs. Renfru thinks it's time to sell."

"Ah." Grant's chin dipped in a single curt signal of understanding. "And the odds of the next building owner being as generous are—"

"Less than stellar."

"I wish I could say otherwise. Are you in a good neighborhood?"

She bobbed her head. "The only reason I got first dibs on my apartment was because one of the women in my yoga class mentioned her friend was getting married and buying a house in the burbs."

"So timing was everything more than once."

Checking her mirrors, she nodded, then faced him with a smile she didn't really feel at the moment. "I guess you could say that."

"What are the odds of timing and a little good luck stepping up to the plate a third time?"

"About the same as me winning the Irish Sweepstakes."

His phone buzzed again and she was sorely tempted to suggest he throw the dumb thing away. Then again, that phone tethering him to business twenty-four seven meant he probably didn't have to worry about where he'd be sleeping at night any time soon.

CHAPTER SIX

"I love this color." Lily stood back from the wall in her soon-to-be bakery and smiled at the man in her life.

Holding a paint roller doused in Summer Blue, Cole looked from the wall to her. "You're sure? This is it?"

"Positive." Originally she'd dreamed of cream colored walls but soon realized color was in order. It had taken ten samples and two days to come up with this shade but she loved it.

"This is it, men." Cole slapped his buddies on the back. Payton and Regan had used their two days off from the fire department to repair and prep the walls for Lily's new bakery.

The front door of what had been the old Boutique on Main Street flew open and Louise Franklin breezed in like a gusty wind. "Your grandmother isn't answering her phone."

"It's the week she and the General go to that specialty yarn shop north of Boston. They probably went today and most likely she left the thing on her dresser, or in the car, or who knows. They should be home soon." Lily and her sisters and cousins had pretty much given up on getting their grandmother to join the modern world and actually use her cell phone.

"Lucy is playing coy too."

"Coy?" Cole repeated.

That was pretty much what Lily had thought. Lucy fit many descriptions but coy wasn't one of them.

Louise nodded, ignoring the patchwork painted wall. "She won't say anything more than that tall, dark and dreamy man with Violet is a new guest at the lake."

Lily drew a blank. What new guest?

"When I saw them crossing the street into the hardware store, well." Had Louise Franklin been wearing pearls, she'd have been clutching them in search of her next words. "I simply had to go say hello. After all, it's been a while since I've seen Violet. And with such a handsome specimen."

No doubt the man had as much if not more to do with her curiosity than spotting Violet in town. "Of course you did. That's the neighborly thing to do."

"I wasn't able to stay long and chat as Tom was ready with my bird seed order. But color me surprised when not more than a shake of a cat's tail after I'd left Betty's, who do I see at the Village Creamery?"

The two firemen prepping to paint the walls paused and looked up at her. She had a pretty good guess that Louise wouldn't have come rushing in this particular storefront if she'd seen anyone other than Violet and this new man.

Before Lily could form a response, Louise had prattled on. "Violet and that very same handsome specimen. Smiling and making goo-goo eyes at each other."

Cole mouthed "goo-goo" to Lily and she stopped herself from rolling her eyes.

"Mabel at the diner says they were spotted walking all over town too. What do you suppose *that's* all about?"

If Lily had any idea who the man was, she might have had some idea how to answer Louise's question. Of course, suggesting Louise go back to the Creamery and ask Violet directly would not be the right response. Too bad for Louise if she expected to find more gossip from Lily. How could Louise see all this construction under way and expect Lily to...wait. What was Lily thinking? Louse Franklin was the town gossip extraordinaire. Of course she'd come to the closest relative actually in the city limits, if not to learn more, than to be the first to spread the news. The only thing Lily could give Louise credit for is that now she was just as curious as the older woman. Why *was* Violet making goo-goo eyes at a stranger?

• • • •

Walking through town, Hart House's newest guest had taken in the shops and residents with sincere interest. So much so that they'd taken a short detour to the next town over before coming home. At this point, he probably knew as much about the two towns and their inhabitants as Violet did. With the sun slowly setting there'd be no time left for him to try out the new jeans and shoes today, though that hadn't seemed to bother him at all. He'd been all smiles all afternoon.

Now, driving the short distance along the main road to the family home, Grant's expression had taken on a more pensive, serious air. Actually, something had shifted ever since they'd climbed into the car and she'd shared about her housing dilemma. "A penny for your thoughts."

Grant's brows lifted and quickly fell. "Haven't heard that in a while. It fits."

"Fits?"

"With this town. The mountain. The way everything seems to be a throwback in time."

"Ah." She turned down the road to the main house. From here there was an amazing glimpse of the lake down the hill. A few more seconds and the view would be obscured by all the trees, but not the house. Even at night that old house stood proud and tall, a testament to whichever great grandfather had taken on construction of the biggest house on the mountain. Of course, it was far from the largest house now, but it was still one of the most impressive. As Grant had said before, a throwback in time.

"More guests?" His gaze fell on the handful of cars parked in front that hadn't been there earlier in the day.

"Maybe." She recognized one of them. Her sister Heather had put her foot down at the hospital and now worked Monday through Friday in Boston and came up to the lake on weekends, barring some emergency where she needed to remain close to a patient. Meanwhile, fundraisers were underway to build a cardiac care unit at the hospital across the lake. Soon, patients would seek Heather and the team out in the pristine Lakeside region, the same way the most complex cases came to Boston.

"Do you mind walking back if I park by my cabin?" She didn't want to take up any more of the limited parking spaces in front of Hart House.

"Not at all." Grant's eyes scanned the few cabins visible from the main house. "Which cabin is yours?"

"Actually, it's my mother's. A wedding gift from the General and Grams. When my mom isn't renovating the thing, my sisters and I will use it to visit the lake. Same thing with my cousin Iris and her sister Zinnia. Their mom's cabin is just across the hill from ours. Aunt Virginia moved into a larger house on the property after Callie was born." Violet rolled down the dirt road and stopped in front of her mom's cabin.

"This does look a little bigger than my cabin."

Violet slammed the car door and resting her arms along the roof line, leveled her gaze with his. "A little?"

"All right," he chuckled, "definitely bigger, but it still blends in well." He came around the car to meet her and for a split second she thought he was going to take her hand.

"Absolutely." Violet turned toward Hart House and followed the path uphill. "The General would not have stood for anything that interferes with the tranquility of the lake. None of us would, really." Close to the house, Violet slowed her steps at the sound of muffled voices and laughter. "Except, of course, for card games."

Even though they had not yet had dinner, it was obvious they'd attracted a crowd for tonight's card game.

● ● ● ●

The sound of gravel spitting under wheels pulled Grant's attention away from the house ahead. He hadn't expected such a crowd.

An attractive redhead exited the passenger door. Something in her smile reminded him of Violet, but he didn't know if that made her a cousin or a sister or just memorable. The two car doors slammed shut, and the man who'd exited the driver side hurried around the hood to meet the woman, their hands easily linking. They fit together well.

"Lily, this is Mr. Whitaker, a guest at Hart Land." Violet waved at the redhead, then gestured toward Grant. "This is my cousin Lily and her fiancé Cole."

That would explain the similar gleams in their eyes and the easy stride matched step for step. If not newlyweds, then engaged was the next best fit. "Nice to meet you, and please call me Grant."

Handshakes and casual greetings aside, Lily looked intently at her cousin before the group turned to move forward, then fell into step beside her, without letting go of the fiancé's hand. "You'll never guess who stopped at the bakery to say hello."

Violet's step faltered slightly as her brows dipped in thought before shaking her head. "I'm too tired to play twenty questions. Who?"

"Louise Franklin. Apparently, she simply could not wait to come and tell me about you and Mr. Whitaker here at the hardware store."

Violet rolled her eyes.

"And the ice cream parlor," Lily added.

"Oh brother," Violet huffed. "The chief gossiper for the Merry Widow's Club must be in hog heaven."

Not used to small towns where everyone supposedly, and apparently did indeed, know everyone's business, Grant couldn't decide from the two women's reactions if this was a bad thing or just a fact of life. He wasn't even going to consider a group called the *Merry Widows*.

"And just to add the cherry topping to your day," Lily followed them up the front steps, "Louise is here to play cards."

Violet paused, gripping Lily's arm. "Oh no. I hope she's not filling Lucy's head with crazy ideas."

Now Grant had his answer. Potentially a problem, and his fault. He didn't like that at all.

"Ha," Lily laughed loudly moving past her cousin. "As if she needed any help. But you should've thought of that before you ordered ice cream with a good-looking stranger."

Together, Lily and Cole hurried up the stairs and fell quickly out of sight. Violet muttered something about 'she should have known better' and Grant was left wondering if Violet considered him good-looking too. He had to shake his head and follow his hostess. He wasn't fifteen and this wasn't some after school party. Maybe it was simply a reflection of yesteryear that lingered from their day together. That had to be what had him reverting momentarily from a successful businessman to a naïve youth.

"There you are." Fiona Hart rose from her seat to greet her granddaughter then sat again, a shopping bag from the specialty shop at her feet. "We were just talking about you."

Violet scanned the immediate area. "I thought I saw Heather's car out front."

"Oh, no." Mrs. Hart shook her head. "We have a new guest. Must be a similar car."

"Oh." Disappointment shone in Violet's eyes.

"It was lovely seeing you in town today." The way the woman he knew to be Louise Franklin grinned at him and Violet—as though she'd caught them skinny dipping in the family pool—he could just bet what they'd been talking about too.

"Violet was nice enough to show me around. Beautiful country you have here."

"Yes, it is." Fiona Hart smiled wistfully. "My family were some of the first people to settle this mountain. Harold's family too."

"They say the families battled over who to name the town after," Louise added.

"Now that's just gossip." The tall man who had buzzed by him earlier in the day made his way over with a spry older fellow from the barber shop at his side. "The Harts and the Lawfords got along like ducks in a pond."

"More like the Hatfields and McCoys," Louise muttered under her breath. From the easy way the skinny old guy jabbed her with his elbow, Grant had a feeling muttering things under her breath wasn't anything new.

A beefy hand shot out in front of him. "Harold Hart. Pleased to meet you."

"Likewise." Grant's grandfather had instilled in him at an early age that much could be discovered about a man from the clasp of his hand. Harold Hart was firm, to the point, and knew how to apply just enough pressure before easing back. Negotiating with this man was going to prove interesting.

"Mr. Whitaker, I mean Grant," Fiona corrected herself, "is staying in the Elm."

"Good choice." The General beamed. "Short walk to the lake."

"He'd probably like the Birch cabin better," another woman wearing a large wrap around apron piped in, coming through the door with a bowl of mixed nuts in each hand. "Better views."

Iris, who had followed Lucy with a tall drink for her

grandmother, leaned into Violet and whispered loud enough for him to make out something like, "Right across from you. Looks like you're it, cuz."

At the same moment, Lily and Violet sucked in a breath with such synchronized precision, he might have thought it had been rehearsed.

"Lucy." The censuring tone in Fiona Hart's voice belied the sweet smile on her face. Coupled with Violet and Lily's reaction, Grant couldn't help but wonder what was all this about?

Lucy simply grinned at her employer, then set the bowls down. One by the General, and one by his wife. "Dinner will be served in about fifteen minutes. You joining us, Ralph? Louise? There's plenty."

"No thanks," Ralph said. "Louise and I are meeting up with Floyd and Thelma for dinner. We'll be back later for a game or two."

Lucy nodded and spun away, Ralph turned in the opposite direction to leave and, lips pressed tightly in a forced smile, poor Louise glanced from the door to Violet and looked about as eager to leave Hart House as a death row inmate to leave his cell.

"Coming?" Ralph hesitated.

Shoulders deflating, Louise nodded and hurried behind her friend.

At the slap of the screen door slamming shut, Grant leaned into Violet, keeping his voice low. "Did I hear correctly?"

"About?" Violet inched closer.

"Louise is going out with Thelma?"

Violet's face pinched as she smothered a laugh. "You heard correctly."

"Should we be worried?" he teased.

"Only if one of them buys a convertible. Until then, we should be safe." Her eyes twinkled brightly, matching a broad smile. A really nice smile.

"Have a seat." The General waved to one of several empty rockers on the enclosed corner of the expansive porch.

"Thanks." Though Grant would have preferred a little alone time to bond with the older man, he'd take whatever options he had and sank into the woven seat beside him. "This is quite a place you have."

"If these walls could talk." The General's already pleasant smile brightened. "Generations of Harts have been brought up in this old house. Some of the secrets we know, others, well…"

"So you grew up here too?" He had to start the conversation somewhere.

"Until the day I left for the Academy. Came home some, but we didn't get summers off like ordinary universities."

"You came home enough." Fiona smiled. "We met the second summer when he came home for two weeks."

"Two weeks?" Grant looked from one spouse to the other.

"Love at first sight," Violet and Lily repeated.

"When you know, you know." The General bobbed his chin, then turned adoring eyes to his wife. "Doesn't take long to realize a rose isn't a dandelion."

"No." Grant chuckled. "When you put it that way, I suppose not."

"We wrote faithfully," the General added.

Fiona picked up her project. "Every week I'd get a letter from my Harold, sometimes twice a week."

"I didn't always have much time, but when it matters, you make the time."

That was something his grandfather had taught him as well. Success is in the details. Whether it was love or business, the key was in the details, and details required time. Which is why Grant was here and not at his office.

"The following year, when Harold came home, he got down on one knee."

The General smiled. "On the point. At sunrise."

"I thought it was sunset?" Lily asked.

Both grandparents shook their head, but it was the grandfather who explained, "Our futures, like the start of a new day, would only grow brighter."

So the old general had a romantic streak. Who knew?

CHAPTER SEVEN

Violet had heard the stories of her grandparents' sort-of whirlwind romance at least a hundred times and it never got old. What neither had mentioned this time around was that the night before the proposal was the then midshipmen's last night at the lake before returning to school. Her grandparents had spent most of the night dancing on the point, and the rest of it roasting marshmallows over an open fire. When the sun peeked over the horizon, her grandfather got down on one knee and asked Fiona Lawford to marry him as soon as he graduated. The story always made her smile.

Car doors slammed and her cousins Cindy and Poppy came running up the porch steps and through the door.

"Where's your mother, dear?" Fiona glanced up from stabbing at the large project draping her lap.

Poppy sat beside her grandmother. "The Bunkers walked in the door just before closing. They want to make changes."

"Again." Cindy rolled her eyes heavenward. "It's families like the Bunkers that make me wish we weren't the only funeral home in the county."

"Now, now." Her grandmother pulled a strip of yarn through the rug she was working on.

At least in this project there was little chance the square rug would contort into an odd shape. Maybe.

"That isn't nice." Grams poked the soon to be rug again.

"Neither are they." Poppy scooped up a handful of nuts. "What's for dinner?"

"Shepherd's Pie."

"Oh, that will hit the spot." Poppy smiled, some of the weariness leaving her expression. "It's been a long day."

"Dinner's ready," Lucy called from inside the doorway.

"Yes." Lily pushed to her feet. "I could eat a rhinoceros."

Finding herself beside their new guest, once again soaking in the conversation around him, Violet wondered where Hart House fit in his plans. "Hungry?"

"Actually," he smiled down at her, "I'm starved. Guess it was all that walking."

Too bad she didn't feel the same way. The more concerned she grew over her housing situation, the less her appetite seemed to hang around.

The vibration from Grant's phone buzzing surprised her. From his wide-eyed expression, she hadn't been the only one. Reception at the house was sketchy at best for some providers. Based on his lack of signal in the cabins she already knew which service he used. "And then again, depending on the server, sometimes the phones work here at the house."

"Fickle." Pulling the cell from his pocket, he glanced down. The bridge of his nose pleated and his eyes narrowed. A quick swipe and whatever had him frowning was brushed away.

"Anything wrong?"

"Hm?" He glanced up, then shook his head. "Just another day in real estate."

She might have believed him except for the fact that by the time they'd made it halfway through dinner, every time the conversation turned away from him, he tapped the pocket holding the phone and the deep frown came back.

"I understand my granddaughter showed you around town today." The General stabbed at his apple pie.

"Yes. Lawford is a tourist's treasure."

"I'm banking on it." Lily dropped her free hand on Cole's and gave a gentle squeeze.

A tiny prick of envy poked at Violet. First her sister Heather and now her cousin had found the perfect man for their lives. Even though Violet's current to-do list only involved a little fun dating—not getting married—watching all these loving couples popping up was enough to have her second guessing herself.

"When will the bakery be opening?" Grant asked.

Lily's eyes lit with excitement. "Just a couple more weeks and we should be done with construction and ready to do business."

"Congratulations." Grant scooped at the last morsel of pie on his plate. "If this is any example of your goods, you should have no trouble bringing in the customers."

"That's what I keep telling myself." The smile that tipped the edges of her cousin's mouth looked a bit shaky.

"For any business to succeed it needs a steady flow of foot traffic." Their guest seemed to be considering his words carefully. "As cute as downtown Lawford is, not that many people besides Violet and me were walking the streets today."

"Things get a little busier on the weekends," Cindy offered. "Even the veterinary clinic has a revolving door on Saturday."

"And the warmer weather brings more people too," Poppy added.

"So, what might help foot traffic during the week, or winter months, is something new to bring more people in the area on a regular basis."

"You mean more tourists?" her grandmother asked.

Grant nodded. "Or residents."

"I don't see a housing boom coming any time soon." The General reached for his coffee cup. "If anything, new money has torn down small clusters of original homes, much like our two bedroom cottages, and replaced them with a single McMansion for only one family."

Grams delicately swiped at each corner of her mouth, then set the napkin on the table. "Maybe something like the Olla Podrida would be nice on this side of the lake."

"Olla Podrida?" Grant asked.

Shaking his head, the General leaned forward. "That would be the specialty shopping and arts center across the lake."

"Yes," Grams said with much more enthusiasm than her husband. "It's specializes in all things arts and crafts. Nora has a wonderful yarn shop. And there's this little gallery that does nothing but watercolors. They even have classes."

Iris pushed away from the table and picked up her grandmother's empty plate along with hers. "Are you thinking of taking up painting too, Grams?"

"Oh, no." The older woman shook her head. "I have my hands

full with this rug for the kitchen, and when I'm done, I have another one planned for the front hall."

Violet eyed the project. Though the square patch seemed to have its shape and size intact, some of the yarn strands seemed to be a bit longer in some places than others. What Violet didn't know was whether that was the way it was supposed to look or if her grandmother had managed to struggle with another craft.

Across the table, his lips pressed tightly together, Grant nodded at her grandmother but from the way he tapped at the phone in his pocket, Violet knew his mind was miles away.

"Well," the General said. "Shall we move this to the other room? The others should be here soon."

Clearing his throat, Grant pushed from the table. "If you'll excuse me, it's been a long day and I have some business to attend to."

The General's jaw fell open and Violet knew poor Grant was about to get the lecture on coming to the lake to unplug, relaxing and communing with nature.

Before her grandfather could utter a word, her grandmother slipped a hand around her husband's elbow and smiled at their guest. "Of course, a busy man like you has a good many things to attend to."

"Thank you for understanding, but I will take a rain check on the card game."

The General nodded. "Any time, son, any time."

"If you don't like cooking, you are welcome to join us for breakfast here at the house tomorrow." Grams leaned into her husband. "Lucy sets a buffet in the dining room starting at eight am."

"That sounds wonderful, and very kind of you." Grant bobbed his head, retreating a few steps before turning and leaving the room.

Funny how the conversation had flowed for hours and yet somehow, she didn't know anything more about his land deal than she had over ice cream. And what was it about his phone that had him looking so glum?

Frowning, the General shook his head. "That man needs a little more time to do nothing. And someone to show him how."

Her grandmother tipped her head to one side, looking up at her husband. "Perhaps we should take advantage of Violet being here and arrange for a little afternoon yoga for anyone who wants to relax."

By anyone, Violet had the feeling her grandmother meant Mr. Grant Whitaker. As if it weren't bad enough that Lucy was always sticking her two cents in to match up people who had no business being together, now her own grandmother was getting into the matchmaking fray. Maybe Violet needed to return to Boston sooner than later.

• • • •

Not bothering to stop at his cabin, Grant briskly walked to the lake edge. Not since that one moment when his phone buzzed at the house had it made another sound. Never had he felt so disconnected from life and reality. Late this afternoon it was a pleasant change. By the time they'd sat down for dinner, his mind raced, second guessing all the things that were, or were not, happening on the job, along with the new plans dancing around all his existing responsibilities.

Normally his phone buzzed, dinged, or rang almost constantly, seven days a week, and almost twenty four hours a day. All this silence was making him nervous. He knew the second his cell picked up a signal. At the sandy edge of the lake his phone started dinging like a slot machine at Vegas. What bothered him more were the almost frantic texts from Madge, his and Joe's executive assistant. For reasons he had yet to figure out, Joe had gone off radar too and Madge was not taking it well.

Maybe he'd find some answers in his email. Even though he preferred to handle correspondence on his laptop with access to a keyboard, the lack of internet in the cabins, wired or otherwise, or a decent signal to use his phone for a hotspot, meant scrolling through emails on his phone. Making do was another fact of life his grandfather had taught him. The night wind slapped at his face. Violet's fire would be a nice touch about now. Pacing to keep warm, he quickly tossed the trivial emails, responded to a few others, but nothing explaining Joe's absence.

Stabbing at the familiar number for speed dial to Joe's private line, Grant waited for his longtime friend and partner to answer.

"Fiorello."

"About time." Hearing the man's voice did wonders to lower Grant's building stress levels.

"Did you sign the deal?" Joe groused. "We don't want word to get out that this puppy is up for sale."

"It's not." As a matter of fact, in only one day, for the first time that he could remember, Grant actually wondered if his own grandfather was totally off base with this lead. Not a single word during dinner had led him to believe the General for even a nanosecond had ever considered leaving Hart Land.

"Well, what are you waiting for?"

Good question. He could probably say if Joe hadn't fallen off the radar siccing Madge on him that right now Grant would be playing cards and schmoozing with the old man instead of pacing on a freezing cold swath of sandy beach. But he really did need to get some internet legwork done. "Where have you been all day?"

"Working. Which is more than I can say about you."

"I'm serious. Madge has been lighting up my phone. Or at least she would if I got decent reception out here."

"Nothing for you or her to worry about. I've got it all taken care of."

"All what taken care of?"

"Listen, I'm wet and tired and up to my eyeballs in plumbing. You let me handle the construction end. You just keep those deals coming. Get the General's signature. Now."

"Joe—"

"I have to go. Celia is shouting supper's getting cold. Stop worrying. I've got this."

Without another word, the phone cut off and Grant didn't like the tightening knot forming deep in his gut. Maybe sleeping on the beach with his laptop wasn't that crazy an idea after all.

CHAPTER EIGHT

Sunrise at the lake was as beautiful as the sunset the night before. No wonder people paid top dollar to do nothing but follow the sun. If not for the disconnect from the outside world, Grant might be able to get used to all this peace and quiet. He glanced at his phone with no reception. *Or not.*

Although, even with the limited data he'd collected while on the beach, he'd been surprised at how much he'd been able to accomplish offline before calling it a night. Now, at the truly crack of dawn, he thanked heavens that the cabin came stocked with strong coffee and travel mugs so he could access the outside world and caffeinate at the same time. Resting on the stone wall that separated the grassy area from the sand, he'd shot off another long list of emails on his phone, pausing only when he noticed the shades of pink painting the sky.

Joe's words from last night lingered in the back of his mind. *"I've got this."* Grant sure as hell hoped so. Something was amiss. He could feel it in his bones. What was that saying about the calm before the storm? Things had been way too calm of late.

Coming to his feet, he slid his phone into his breast pocket. Even if he knew it wouldn't be any use to him in most areas around Hart Land, the illusion of remaining connected did wonders for his peace of mind. He'd rather walk down Main Street naked than leave his phone behind. Turning, he marched back to his cabin for a refill of roasted fuel.

Near his front door, he spotted the General standing on the Hart House porch up the hill. Alone. Coffee didn't seem as important as it had only seconds ago. Following the cobbled path to the front drive, Grant kept his eye on the figure in the distance. Standing at the railing, a golden retriever perched at either side of him, the General seemed lost in the horizon. Still in his bathrobe, the figure didn't seem as stern or strong as he had the day before. This morning, his countenance reflected that of a man who was indeed older and tired and perhaps ready to move on from the responsibility of running a family legacy.

About to call out as he got closer to the porch steps, Grant hesitated when he noticed the older man popping something in his mouth and chasing it with a long swallow from the glass in his hand. Grant's footsteps on the wooden stairs must have alerted the General to his presence. Immediately, the military man came to life. His shoulders straightened and eyes, lost in thought only a moment ago, sharpened. Casually, he slipped an amber prescription pill bottle into his pocket. "An early riser. Always a good thing."

"Catching the worm and all that." He gestured toward the General's pocket. "Feeling under the weather?"

The older man raised a brow and then slowly lowered it in place and sighed. "Fit as a fiddle. Tell a doctor your age and they'll give you an antibiotic in case you get sick."

This time Grant was the one to raise a questioning brow. Weren't they living in an era where doctors were trying to reverse the over prescribing of antibiotics?

The old man shifted his weight. "There's a fresh pot of coffee brewing inside. Like your coffee strong?"

"Yes." He nodded. "As a matter of fact, I do."

"Good. Good." Harold Hart's lips curled up with a pleased grin, almost as if the two of them now shared some unique secret. Which, of course, made no sense at all. "Lady, Sarge." Turning on his heel, the General led the way into the house, both dogs keeping pace beside him. Tails wagging, one glanced up at him and the way his head dipped, he could have made an argument that the animal nodded at him. Maybe the dog needed a strong cup of coffee too.

• • • •

No matter how much Violet stretched, deep breathed, or meditated this morning, she simply could not find her Zen. Despite the early end to an evening of card playing, and the country quiet that came with sleeping at the lake, unlike the night before, she tossed and turned chasing sleep. Her morning yoga routine usually energized her. Not today. Not even her favorite CD with the sounds of waves crashing had helped. She suspected the only thing that was going to help would be securing a new permanent location for her studio. She didn't even want to think what was going to happen with her apartment.

Though it wasn't part of her usual routine, like it or not, if she wanted to stay awake during daylight hours, some of Lucy's high octane coffee was in order. Pulling the collar of her jacket higher around her ears to fight the morning chill, she hurried up the walk and took the porch steps two at a time. If only Mother Nature would make up her mind. One day Violet could feel an early spring creeping along, and the next, winter reared its bitter head again.

"I was wondering when you would be showing your pretty face around here." Grinning like a kitten with a belly full of cream, Lucy passed Violet on her way to the dining room. "Our guest has been keeping your grandfather company for well over an hour. I didn't think you were ever going to get here."

The admission alone was almost enough to make Violet retrieve her coat from the rack and hurry back out the door, not stopping till she reached Boston. Lucy's matchmaking efforts always, absolutely always, led to trouble. If she hadn't actually been looking forward to breakfast with Grant and her family, she would have definitely turned right around.

"Don't look so horrified." Iris came off the bottom step from the upstairs rooms. "She's actually doubling up on her bets."

"Excuse me?"

"Lucy thinks he might be a good fit for Martha. Just in case there aren't sparks flying, she's got Martha's mom on speed dial. Poor Mabel, as if running a diner isn't work enough, now she has to contend with Lucy."

"I suppose at least Lucy won't be setting the house on fire over this."

Iris chuckled. "I know it wasn't funny at the time, but you have to admit the woman has a talent."

"For creating havoc, definitely. For matchmaking, not so much."

"Come on," Iris linked elbows with her, "today's my last day here. Let's see if I can't help deflect cupid's arrow."

"If Cupid is our Lucy, the woman isn't using an arrow, she's probably using a harpoon."

"Don't you two bring back memories?"

Arms still linked, the two cousins turned at the sound of their grandmother's voice.

"When you girls were little there were always two or three of you at a time, huddled together and sharing secrets." Grams sidled up beside Violet, and like Iris, slipped her arm under Violet's, linking their elbows. "I want you to know your grandfather and I are very happy that lately all of you girls have been here more often."

"Me too," they both echoed.

Her grandmother was right. In all the traveling she'd done with her family through the years, nothing compared to time at the lake.

"Now if we could only get Zinnia to escape for a few days." Grams shook her head.

"I've tried," Iris said softly. "Really I have. But this new venture of hers has her head to the grindstone twenty-four seven."

"Yes." Grams sighed. "I'll have to think on that one."

"And there they are." The General stood as his wife and granddaughters entered the room. "We've been holding off on diving in until you arrived."

Without missing a beat, Grant pushed to his feet as well. "Good morning."

A round of "good morning" circled the room as dishes and silverware clattered, food was scooped up from the buffet, and everyone settled in again at the table.

"Did you sleep well?" Grams addressed Grant.

He spread the napkin across his lap. "Yes, ma'am."

"Wonderful." Grams took a sip of juice and dabbed at the corners of her mouth. "Do you have plans for today?"

"I was just talking to the General about the possibilities."

"That's right." The General nodded at Grant. "Now that he has the right attire, I thought it would be nice to take him for a hike on some of the trails and show him the property more thoroughly."

"Good idea, dear. The exercise will do you good. Just don't overdo it."

The General shot his wife a sly grin. "I'm still a Marine."

All Grams did was smile up at her husband, but her eyes repeated her warning. In response, Gramps bestowed her with an adoring gaze and sweet smile.

"The General was kind enough to make the suggestion after I mentioned that normally I work out every other day. Skipping two days in a row, a long walk will do me good."

"Oh," Grams practically sang, "I'm so glad you said that."

Holding a fork full of scrambled eggs, Grant's hand froze midway to his mouth. "Said what?"

"That you need more exercise." Grams turned to Violet. "Your grandfather and I had an excellent idea last night. Since you're not able to go home to work for a little while, you could give a yoga class or two here at the lake."

Even though this wasn't the first time her grandmother had set up an impromptu yoga class on an extended visit, Grams actually looked quite excited about the idea. Too bad Violet was afraid to find out what any of that might have to do with Grant Whitaker.

"As it happens," her grandmother continued without skipping a beat, "I took the liberty of posting a notice for some of our guests and then phoning a few friends."

Those three words—*a few friends*—had Violet literally teetering nervously on the edge of her seat, waiting to hear exactly what the woman had planned.

"You, young man," Fiona Margaret Lawford Hart spun about to face Grant, "are the linchpin to the entire plan."

Oh, Violet did not like the sound of that. And judging by the way Grant's fork continued to hang in mid-air, he probably thought the same thing.

Grams stretched her arm out and let her hand fall on Grant's. "You see, thanks to my dear friend Louise and her big mouth, there is not an able-bodied female in this town who doesn't want to meet you."

The loud clank of Grant's fork dropping to its plate wasn't enough to drag all gazes away from Violet's grandmother.

Bubbling with excitement, Grams turned from Grant to face Violet. "You already have six women signed up for this morning's class."

"Today?" Violet's voice came out barely above a whisper.

"Yes, dear. I didn't know how much time you'd need to prepare, or if you want to rearrange something in the parlor. I told everyone early afternoon, two o'clock." She turned back to Grant. "And since you need a replacement for your regular exercise routine, Violet's yoga class will be perfect. So it's a win-win for everyone."

"Brilliant suggestion." The General smiled at his wife. "You'd have made an excellent officer. Your ability to organize at the drop of a hat is priceless."

"That's why it took 10,000 men to replace me, dear."

"That it did, yes sir." The General redirected his attention to Grant. "After your workout with Violet will be the perfect time to take to the trails. Show you all we have to offer our guests."

"I look forward to the exercise, and," Grant spoke slowly, facing Grams, clearly searching for words, "the yoga sounds like a… wonderful idea as well."

The entire idea sounded like a lot of things to Violet, but wonderful wasn't one of them.

Grams enthusiastically rubbed her hands together. "Now, I have a lovely pair of pink flannel pants that I bought for just such an occasion."

"Oh, what a shame." Grant snapped his fingers, his expression brightening. "I didn't bring any workout clothes. I'm afraid I'm going to have to pass on the yoga class, but thank you for thinking of me."

"Nonsense." Even though her plate was more than half full, Grams closed her knife and fork and stood up. "We have lots of miscellaneous items in the lost and found. I'm sure something will fit."

"Lost and found?" he repeated, abandoning any pretense of eating breakfast.

Grams nodded. "A closet full. I never throw anything out."

Violet's mind drifted back a day to the man standing beside the expensive sports car in an outfit suitable for a page in the Neiman Marcus catalog. No way could she picture Grant in hand me down attire.

"Let's see what we've got. I'll be right back." Her grandmother waltzed out of the room.

Grant's gaze bounced from Violet to the General and back. If he was looking for help, he was out of luck. Her grandmother was a force to be reckoned with. Once she made up her mind, good, bad, or ugly, there would be no changing it. Certainly not one of her granddaughters and as far as the General was concerned, his wife walked on water. When it came to Fiona Hart, there was no such thing as a bad idea.

"Who's ready for more?" Carrying a fresh tray of bacon, Lucy came to a stop at the table, her forehead creasing at the sight of Gram's half eaten plate. "Is something wrong?"

"Not at all," the General answered. "Fiona is off gathering some exercise clothes for our guest. He's going to sit in on a yoga class with Violet."

"Is he now?" Lucy's grin was almost blinding.

"Here we go." With a smile to match the housekeeper's, Grams came in with a pile of neatly folded clothes in her arm and set them on the empty space beside Grant. "These are all the shorts that I think could fit. Well, there was a pretty pair of fuchsia ones by one of those basketball companies." She glanced up a second. "The one I mean has the funny swoopy thing. Anyhow, you don't look like a fuchsia man, but," she returned to unfolding the shorts and laying them out on every empty space, "I do believe they would look wonderful on you."

Violet probably should have gone with her. A woman who wore vibrant colors with the flair of a nineteen sixties go-go dancer probably shouldn't have been tasked with picking out clothes for a man who probably sent his underwear to the dry cleaners. "Let me see what you've got."

"Stand up, please." Grams stepped back, holding a pair of shorts in each hand.

Without hesitating, Grant stood in front of Violet's grandmother. She had to give him credit, the glassy gaze was gone and now he stood calmly as Grams held out two hideous pairs of shorts.

"I think this is the one." Grams grinned up at him. "Yes, these will do just fine."

Grant actually smiled and nodded. The way he held the clothes her grandmother handed off to him, anyone would think he was delighted with the ensemble.

The man was either a fantastic actor or the nicest man she'd ever met. And heck if she had a clue which one was true.

CHAPTER NINE

How she had gotten talked into this Violet did not know. Not that she didn't love teaching yoga, she did, but she knew darn well that the women coming today couldn't have cared less about improving their flexibility or balance. Her grandmother could have just as easily invited them to come sit in the parlor, drink margaritas and drool over Grant from a distance.

Violet didn't look up as the pocket door slid open. Hand behind her shoulder, tugging at the elbow by her ear with the opposite hand, she counted to five and brought both arms to her side, then stood to greet the first attendee. To her surprise, Grant stood in khakis, loafers, and a polo shirt that fit like a glove.

"Changed your mind?"

"Not at all. I just didn't think it was terribly prudent to walk over here in shorts and a T-shirt and my bare feet in this weather." He looked left then right. Setting his sights on the large Victorian sofa in the opposite corner, he crossed the room.

"You know, you don't have to do this." She didn't know why she was trying to talk him out of it. She'd actually been looking forward to sharing something she enjoyed with him.

Kicking off his shoes, he unbuckled his belt. "Even though you can't possibly compare a yoga session to a full workout—"

"Can't compare, huh?" Her chin lifted both in indignation and an effort to keep her gaze level with his.

"Well, no." Grant's pants slid to the floor, exposing burnt orange shorts her grandmother had picked out for him. "Lifting weights is much more strenuous than bending over to touch your toes."

Oh, did he have a thing or two to learn about stretching those hamstrings.

"Basically, your grandmother is such a nice lady with good intentions that I simply didn't have the heart to let her down. Especially when she mentioned she'd already gotten people on board to participate."

"So you don't expect a good workout, or mind being ogled by a bunch of seasoned ladies?"

"Excuse me?"

She decided quickly to let her workout speak for itself and stick with her grandmother's idea. Though now that Violet thought about it, having him in a yoga class sounded way more like a Lucy idea. "Remember, you're the linchpin."

Grant froze, his arms up, his shirt lifting off. "She was serious?"

"Yeah." She held back a giggle. "You met Louise."

"She's coming?"

"Yep. So is Thelma, Katie from the One Stop, Nadine Baker who still works part time as police dispatcher—her husband is another one of my grandfather's cronies, Mabel from the diner, one of the guests, and of course Grams."

"Oh yes, the pink pants."

"Yeah. The woman wears a variety of bright colors well."

"I'm thankful she at least picked out sort of matching colors for me."

"Any woman who can't remember what the *swooping thingy* logo is won't have noticed that your tops are from a Texas university and your bottoms are from an Oklahoma university. All she probably noticed was similar shades of orange. Though you should probably be thankful she didn't play mix-and-match the color schemes. You could have wound up mixing maroon or green with that orange."

"At least I can be sure that no universities that I know of have neon pink for their colors."

"Hello!" Not surprisingly, dressed in sweats from a popular clothing store, Louise was the first person besides Grant to arrive. Casually dropping her bag to one side, she pretended rather poorly not to notice Grant in the corner shedding the last of his clothes. "This is such a marvelous idea. I am so glad your grandmother included me."

"Yes. A wonderful idea."

Two more women could be heard giggling and chatting before strolling in, side-by-side.

"Aren't you a pretty sight?" Katie O'Leary came straight to Violet, oblivious to the handsome man standing to one side of the room. "Top of the morning to you."

"And the rest of the day to you." One of her favorite things about growing up in Lawford and going to the One Stop for candy or soda, was visiting with Katie and learning about her Irish heritage. Including the proper greeting and response. The woman was a treasure. If there was such a thing as angels walking among us, Katie O'Leary had to be one of them.

"Your Irish ancestors would be proud of you." Katie gave her a big hug before noticing Grant moving in their direction. "And isn't it nice to have you here with us this morning."

"I assure you, the pleasure is all mine."

And just like that Violet was absolutely positive that had Grant wanted to sell Katie the Blarney Stone, she would have bought it from him no questions asked.

Wearing snug fitting leggings on her bird-like legs and a baggy T-shirt to her knees, Nadine Baker hurried in the door, a yoga mat tucked under her arm. "This sucker has been stored under my staircase for too long." She laughed and gave Grant a quick once over before rolling the mat out on the floor. "And Ned said I was never going to use it."

A few more minutes and everybody was lined up on their yoga mats in front of Violet, including her grandmother in a flaming pink pair of yoga pants and matching top. There wasn't anyone else who she could think of that would get away with that outfit and still exude classic elegance as well as her grandmother.

"All right ladies, let's get started." Like a gaggle of teenage girls, more than one person giggled at her faux pas. "Excuse me, ladies and gent," she corrected.

"And a handsome gent he is," her grandmother chimed in.

"First, we'll warm up." Considering, with the exception of herself and Grant, everyone in the room was old enough to be her grandmother, or at least her mother's older sister, she went with the simple list options. Though for Grant she would've preferred to have him doing a simplified jumping jack, in consideration of the ladies, she opted for a double sidestep, left arm swing, right arm swing instead. Thirty seconds and she moved onto the next one, and the next, and the next. Nadine and Louise were having way too much fun swirling their extended arms in circles.

"That's right. Heat up those shoulders, and now reverse," Violet instructed.

Shifting from forward to backward, Louise cracked jokes about take off and landing.

Last person between the group and the far windows, Grant followed her every instruction to the letter without complaint or comment.

"Time to stretch. We'll start on the hamstrings. Bend forward at the hips and touch the ground. Nice and easy." She stepped forward, strolling past each person, gently adjusting one position or other. "Not too rough. If you can't reach the floor, rest your hands on your thigh or calf. You don't want to pop a hamstring or the party will be over."

"This is like a party, isn't it?" Thelma cooed with delight. "Much more fun than playing Mahjong at Louise's."

"That's only because you never win," Louise shot back.

Since none of these ladies had touched their toes in ages, and the only time Grant had probably ever bent over to touch his toes would have been to tie those expensive Italian shoes of his, after a few more poses, she cut the session about fifteen minutes shy of a normal class.

"This is enough for one day." She closed her hands in front of her, palm to palm. "It's been lovely."

"Yes, it has." Mabel, who had been pretty quiet the whole time, had mostly cast a sideways glance in Grant's direction and quickly looked back. Probably wondering if Lucy's idea of Grant and Martha would be a good one. Then again, Mabel wouldn't be the first person in the room sucked in by those baby blues. "I'd have thought with all the trays I carry, my arms would be in better shape. Are we going to do this again?"

Again?

"Of course we can." Grams, who credited her straight stance and easy gait to her own version of yoga stretches, rolled her shoulders and smiled at Mabel. "Yoga is good for the body and soul."

"So is wine," Louise spoke up. "I put a bottle of pinot in the fridge. Who's in?"

Several voices echoed, "I am."

Wine and yoga? Violet should have thought of that a long time ago.

"So," Mabel slipped on her shoes, "day after tomorrow too soon?"

Caught off guard, Violet had to think a moment. Why not? She couldn't do anything in Boston until she found a new studio. "That'll be fine."

"Same bat time, same bat channel?" Thelma giggled at her retro TV reference.

"Yes, ma'am."

Nadine slung her bag over her shoulder and looked to Grant. "Join us for a glass of wine?"

He flashed a killer smile and slowly shook his head. "I'm afraid I can't. I've agreed to a meeting with the General."

"Next time," the ring leader for the Merry Widows said.

Lucy popped her head in the doorway. "Anyone who's interested, wine in the library. Also, Lily dropped off her diet friendly brownies and a loaf of chocolate chip banana bread."

A synchronized moan filled the room.

"Only one?" Nadine muttered as the ladies hurried past Lucy.

Waiting until they were all out of the room, Lucy looked to Violet. "The General is tied up on one of his group conference calls. Said for you to take Grant here for that property tour. He left a couple of bicycles ready for you on the back porch if you'd like."

"Conference call?" Violet asked. Since when did retired Generals have conference calls.

"You know how your grandfather is with that computer face thing. Ever since he's discovered social media he loves to chat with someone or other. Last week when I brought him his afternoon espresso he had some old goat from Texas on the screen."

Violet nodded and spun to face the only other person in the room. "If you'd rather wait for the General—"

"No. A walk, or ride, will be nice."

"Very well. I'll meet you at the back door in thirty minutes."

Grant nodded. "Thirty minutes."

"You may want to wear pants." Lucy pointed at him and then spinning around to leave, shot over her shoulder, "Those Merry Widows can be a wild bunch after a bottle of wine."

From the other side of the room she noticed Grant biting back a laugh. At least he was keeping his sense of humor. Though, she freely admitted, from the wardrobe and the car and the workaholic vibes she picked up on, a good sport with a sense of humor was not what she'd expected from him. Maybe now she'd find out what else was hiding behind that very pristine, and expensive, veneer.

• • • •

Shoe strings taut, Grant tied the ends and slowly straightening, gingerly pushed to his feet. Less than twenty minutes after what was supposed to have been an effortless workout, both of his legs and his lower back were protesting loudly. "How did that happen?" he mumbled to an empty cabin. He wasn't new to the old adage *no pain no gain*, but even after a strenuous exercise routine, not till the next day would he feel the pain.

Having managed to sneak in a couple of minutes on the beach to check email before changing, at least knowing things he'd set in motion were moving along nicely offset a few of the aches and pains. Well, most things. Madge still seemed a bit out of sorts. Leaning left, then right, he stretched, shook off the discomfort, and took the nearby path back to Hart House. The bright sunshine went a long way to warming the afternoon, but the chilling breeze wasn't optimal for a bike ride. He wasn't sure what the General had been thinking.

The closer he got to the house, the louder the laughter from inside sounded. Following the path around to the back, through the window he could see the ladies inside. Mrs. Hart was the only one seated, working on something in her lap. The other ladies were on their feet, talking, laughing, as Thelma and Louise swayed to a Beatles melody. He didn't know which was more interesting, that there actually were two friends in this town named Thelma and Louise, or that he seemed to be the only one feeling the affects of the afternoon yoga session.

"There you are." Violet stepped off the back porch, rubbing her hands together. Her smile as warm as the afternoon sun.

Any disappointment over missing out on another chance to be alone with the General and hammer home the idea of selling slid away at the sight of that smile.

"It's a bit windy for a bike ride." She turned, leading the way to the back door. "We could walk…" Her voice trailed off slightly.

He waited a beat and then coaxed, "Or?"

Violet's smile gave way to a soft laugh. He liked that too. "We could take my grandfather's Jeep."

Grant raised a silent prayer that he wouldn't have to be hiking all over the county today.

"Though it's not as pretty as walking the trails, the old roads make it easier to cover more territory."

"How about a compromise?"

One brow raised higher than the other. "Such as?"

"A short walk and a longer drive?"

"That can be arranged." She nodded. "How about we walk the shoreline a bit then double back for the Jeep?"

"That'll work." Out of sheer habit, he tapped his pocket, ensuring he had his cell with him.

"There's one catch."

His gaze darted to the waterline in the distance and back. "What would that be?"

"Turn off your phone."

CHAPTER TEN

"What?"

"Your phone." Violet waved a single finger at him. "I know it's in your breast pocket. You keep tapping it like a drummer on caffeine."

"But the best reception is on the shore. I've got calls in to—"

She held up her hand, cutting him off and trying not to laugh at how much his eyes resembled a bugeye cartoon. "There is no way to appreciate the value of the lake's calming quiet, communing with Mother Nature, never mind finding your own inner peace, with that contraption ringing every five seconds."

"It doesn't ring that much." His hand lifted and abruptly dropped to his side again.

"See. You don't even realize how often you reach for it, do you?" She let a hint of a smile show through to soften the near accusation. After all, what did it matter to her if he had his phone or not?

"Okay. Maybe it does ring a bit more than the average persons." He shook his head. "You know, of all the things you might have asked me to do before taking a walk, turning off my phone had not been even on the perimeter of my mind's possibilities."

"It's the lake. One of the last places in the world you can disconnect from the hectic and the crazy. You're here. You might as well enjoy the ride."

His brows dipped into a perfect V. "Wasn't that an old James Taylor song?"

"What?" She was pretty good at following odd threads of conversations. She had to be with an extended family of almost all women, but prepped for more of an argument, she'd lost him.

"What you just said about might as well enjoy the ride. Sounds like a song."

"I have no idea. You're lucky I know who James Taylor is."

Grant turned the power off on his phone, slid it back into his pocket, and began walking. "He was one of my mom's favorite singers. I forget not everyone grew up with a mom stuck in the seventies."

A sharp rumble of laughter escaped unfettered. "My mom was a wanna-be hippie as a kid. I probably know every hit Peter Paul and Mary ever had. James Taylor may not have been famous during the counter-culture, but he kept the simple folk sound popular for decades. Especially when Mom had control of the tunes in the car."

"So we have more than just military grandfathers in common?" His smile brightened. A nice smile.

"I guess we do."

They reached the edge of the wall that separated the grassy area from the sandy shore.

"Which way do we go?" he asked.

Spinning left, she stuck her arm straight out. "This way. The shore jets in and out with the occasional natural obstacle. This way is the easier walk."

"Easy sounds good."

She didn't try to hide another gurgle of laughter. "Are you really that sore?"

"Let's just say I will never make fun of yoga again." He kept his hands in his pockets and she wondered if it was a conscious effort to stop himself from reaching for that phone.

"You should stretch more. Building muscle is fine, but stretching is important too."

"So I'm noticing."

They walked a few more yards in silence. The sun warmed her back and made the water glimmer. She loved the lake. As far as she was concerned it was the most peaceful place on earth.

His eyes drifted from the water to the land thick with trees and the occasional cabin. "Do you ever walk just the waterline of your grandfather's property?"

"Not usually. It goes pretty far."

"Yes. It does." His lips pressed together and his gaze focused on an unknown point in the distance. He paused and reached to the ground, picking up a stone.

Violet inched closer. "Looking for something in particular?"

His fingers rubbed along the surface of a few stones in his hands. "Flat."

"Okay. Any reason in particular?"

"You ever skip stones?"

Had she? She almost barked out a loud laugh, before shaking her head at him. "Those won't do."

"I think this one's pretty good." He tossed it in the air and caught it. A confident grin taking over his face.

"You're not flipping a coin over a football game." Scanning the scattered stones close to the waterline, she spotted what she was looking for. "This," she proudly held up a stone, "is the things champions are made of."

Those beautiful blue eyes, sparkling like the sun on the lake, bore into her. "Champions?"

"Hold the record at the lake." Her shoulders straightened and she lifted her chin, bringing her to her full height. All five foot six and three quarters of it. "Never been broken."

"That you know of." Still grinning, with a shift in weight and a flick of his wrist he sent a stone flying only to sink into the lake like, well, a proverbial stone. "That was just practice."

"Uh huh." Rubbing the stone she held, checking the weight in her palm, she shook any tension from her shoulders. It had been years since she'd done this. Angling her body just right against the shore, she flicked her wrist and elbow, sending the stone dancing along the water.

"Wow. Ten, eleven." He turned to face her before the stone finished skidding along the surface. If his smile grew any wider he might blind people on the other side of the lake. "Pretty good, Champ."

"Nah." Delightful energy fizzled to the surface. "My record is twenty-four."

"And if any of us made it to ten we were having a good day." He reached for another stone, this time weighing more carefully, then turned and flung the stone away from him.

"Five, six, seven. Oops." Even though she actually felt a little sorry for the lackluster performance, she couldn't stop smiling. She was having fun. A lot of fun. And couldn't have been more surprised to be having it with Mr. Fancy Car doing something as simplistic as skimming stones. "Not bad."

"It's coming back to me." He fiddled with another stone. "Considering I haven't done this since I was ten years old at Camp Tawakoni, I feel confidant in saying it could be worse."

"It can always be worse." She laughed and flung another stone. When was the last time she'd had this much fun just hanging out with a guy?

After at least ten stones a piece, the initial rivalry faded to cheers and encouragements and more fun than she'd had in too damn long.

"That's fifteen." Violet waited for Grant's last stone to stop and sink before throwing a fist pump in the air. "Best of the day."

"That was pretty good." A grin broke across his face. "Your turn."

Loosening her grip on the stone in her hand, she inched forward, eyed the distance, gave the stone one last gentle caress and let it slide out of her fingers.

Together they counted one, two. When the stone got to twenty, she felt the adrenaline rush of record-breaking material.

With every skip, Grant inched closer, counting along side her. "Twenty-one, twenty-two."

"Twenty-three, twenty-four, twenty-five!" Both fists in the air, she swung around as it slid to a final twenty-six count and sank under the surface. "I broke my record!"

"Hooyah!" Grant's eyes danced with joy, maybe even pride.

Channeling the giddy little girl who played for hours with friends on the shore, she turned her wrists, holding her hands palm out, delighted when Grant's hands slapped against hers. The contact was sharp and brief, then suddenly, as quickly as the skipping stone had slid under the water's surface, the air grew thick.

Adrenaline pumping through her system turned warm, easily battling the chill of the day. It took her mind an extra beat to shake free of the electricity urging her to move in closer. She already knew the power of those deep baby blues, and woefully unprepared for the equally strong pull of even the briefest touch, like the sensible woman she'd grown into, Violet quickly turned away.

Bending down to hide her fluster, she slowly regained her composure, searching for one more stone. Her heart beat normal and her breath steady, she dared straighten, ready to return to the lighthearted fun of a few minutes ago. Met by the stern set of his jaw, tight press of his lips, and intensity of his gaze, an instinctive sense of self-preservation had her taking a step back.

Grant's eyes didn't waver or hide the internal battle waged behind them. Long seconds ticked by and she could almost swear in a court of the law the exact moment he seemed to make up his mind. "I can't do this."

As if she wasn't already confused enough, his words sent her thoughts into a tail spin. Already unsure of what to make of any of this, she opted to smile and make light of the crazy exchange. "Are you going to tell me you're really the world champion incognito?"

"No." He sucked in a deep breath and made a weak attempt at a smile. "There's something you need to know."

She nodded. Not at all sure she agreed that she wanted to know anything he might have to say. What she wanted was to return to the laughter and joy of minutes ago.

"The property I got a tip that it will be coming up for sale is Hart Land."

"Is that all?" Relief that his darkened expression had nothing to do with them, not that there was a them, she tossed the last stone she held in her hand, watching without counting. "I know that."

"How?"

Violet swiveled in place, smiling up at him. "I may like to keep life simple, but I'm not stupid."

"I certainly didn't think you were."

"Frankly, a child could most likely have put the pieces together. First, you don't stay at the Inn across the lake that has room service and a restaurant in-house. Second, you've willingly spent almost two days here without any effort to leave Hart property. Third, you're casually sucking up to the General—"

"I am not sucking up."

"No? What do you call smiling and ahing at over an hour of old war stories? For us it's love, but you?"

"It's called pre-negotiation recognizance."

"Mm hm." She nodded, holding back a knowing smile.

Chuckling, he brushed the sandy dust from his hands. "Remind me never to underestimate you again. Do you know when your grandfather is thinking of selling?"

"He's not." She pointed to a narrow dirt path ahead, nestled between a clump of trees. "We should head back to the house."

He fell in step beside her. "Please don't be upset with me."

"I'm not upset." She shrugged. Right now, a bundle of emotions were breaking free inside her but none of them had anything to do with a silly notion that he could buy Hart Land.

"Then you wouldn't mind if the General sells?"

She stopped and turned to face him. "Of course I'd mind. But it's a moot point. He's not going to sell."

"Last night I might have agreed with you. But this morning," he hefted one shoulder in a lazy shrug, "your grandfather reminded me more of a man who was ready to move on."

"Nonsense." She turned and kept walking, almost laughing over her shoulder, "Never going to happen."

"I don't know. If he's interested, it could be a sweet deal for a man of his age."

Slowing, she pointed to some raised roots beside her. "Watch your step, and I'm telling you, it's never going to happen."

"And if it does?"

Stopping dead in her tracks, she hefted her hands onto her hips and shook her head at him. "You are stubborn. I don't know what you think happened this morning, but as sure is my name is Violet Preston, my grandfather would never sell this land. So, if you still want a ride to see the property, we need to get moving. But just remember I told you first, it's never going to happen."

• • • •

"If you don't mind a little detour, it's getting late and there's a great spot up the hill to watch the sunset."

The sentence was the longest Violet had strung together since climbing into the Jeep with him. Down by the shore, when she'd slapped him a double-handed high five, something inside him seemed to snap. At that second, he knew holding back the truth of his mission was a risk he was unwilling to take. Until this moment he'd been second guessing the wisdom of that decision. "I'd like that." *Really like that.*

"This next part can get a bit bumpy."

He thought the last hour had already been. "I can handle bumpy."

Not far ahead she turned off the gravel drive and onto what looked more like a ditch than a road. Good thing they used the Jeep, and darn good thing Grant didn't try to maneuver this dirt road in his convertible. Bouncing up the road he reminded himself that Hart Land was the biggest piece of single owner lakefront parcel. What he'd clearly underestimated from the maps is exactly how much land came with the Hart name.

Having bounced most of the way up the hill, the vehicle came to a stop on a narrow landing. Tree trunks with a smattering of green branches was the only thing he could see. Not a sunset in sight.

"This is where we get out and walk."

He nodded and hopped out of the car, a bit more slowly than he might have only a day before.

A low rumble of laughter escaped before she hid it behind a soft smile. "I probably should have warned you that men often suffer from tightness, particularly in the hips, hamstrings, and shoulders that can lead to soreness when first given a good workout."

"I wouldn't have believed you anyway."

"There is that." Her smiled brightened, then she turned away.

He was happier than he should have been to see it again.

A few minutes later she stopped and turned to face him. "You doing okay?"

"So far so good." The climb wasn't steep, but not enough people came through here to leave a worn path. Nature in its pristine beauty. Grant wasn't sure he could say that about any place else he'd ever been. Even the most beautiful cliffsides of Hawaii had in some way or form been contaminated by too many humans.

"Just a few more feet."

At the top of the hillside, a flat plateau the size of a small room came into view, and along with it a panorama that would steal any mere mortal's breath. "Wow."

"I know."

Across the narrow valley the sun had already begun to fall, the bright yellows breaking way to shades of orange and pink along its edges. "This is amazing."

Brushing the sides of her arms, Violet blew out a small breath and backing up, sat on a smooth log. "I could sit here for hours, even in the cold."

Even he might be persuaded to give up his phone and the chaos of work for an extended stay at a view like this. Especially with this tour guide. Which begged a whole new question. Was it the view or the company that made everything about Hart Land so special? Taking a few steps around nature's bench, he noticed the carvings on the back. Initials. Lots of them. "Do local kids trek up here often?"

Her gaze dropped from the horizon to where he'd been looking. "No. Those are all family."

"Family?" His eyelids strained to open wider.

"Yep. Every couple for as far back as Harts have lived on this land." She extended her hand to one corner. "These here," her fingers rubbed gingerly over the RH and TP, "Mom and Dad."

He nodded.

"Over here," her fingers shifted, "this is Aunt Virginia, and on the opposite edge of the knot is Aunt Marissa."

"What about your grandparents?"

Violet smiled. "Over here." Immediately her fingers brushed over four large initials entwined almost center of the log.

"There has to be at least a hundred sets of initials." Maybe more.

"I told you. Every Hart, and the love of their life, is engraved on this log."

"Do you know them all?"

"Most." Her fingers slowly tracing the letters, she recited the names of great grandparents and aunts and uncles. Apparently every child born with the name Hart got to carve his or her initials with their love upon their wedding day.

"The story is Jeremiah Hart, the first settler on the mountain, cleared this patch of land, and taking one of the downed trees, sanded and smoothed the top so the love of his life, Abigail, could sit and enjoy the view. We're not sure what exactly she'd been afflicted with, but we know that he carried her up here when she could no longer walk, and held her when she could no longer sit."

"Sounds like a lot of love."

"That's how the story goes. They had eight children who lived to adulthood. All of their initials are also on this log."

"That certainly explains why there are so many."

"And that's keeping in mind that some generations had very few children. Gramps is an only son of an only son. And my great great grandfather was the only Hart to remain on Hart land. His sisters all married men from other states. Only one sister, Elizabeth, lived here long enough to have her and her husband's initials carved on the family log."

"So what you're saying is a good genealogist could use this log much the way some families use a bible."

"Exactly."

Try as hard as he might, he could not for the life of him remember what his own grandfather's parents' names were. Or his mother's. He knew both sets of grandparents were only children, well, his mom had said that her mother was the only child to make it to adulthood. But whether his great grandparents had had two or ten children he didn't know. And not until this very minute did he think that was a darn shame.

CHAPTER ELEVEN

Staring into the distance, lyrics Violet had heard a very, very long time ago came to mind. "Secret of Life."

"Excuse me?" Grant dragged his gaze away from the pink sky to face her.

"That's the name of the James Taylor song you were thinking of. The song is about enjoying the passing of time."

Grant nodded. "That's right. *Any fool can do it.* Now I remember."

Any fool. Maybe that explained how she, of all people, wound up sitting at the top of Eagle Point with a guy who could steal her breath away. The only thing more surprising than discovering a playful side to Mr. All Business, was seeing his appreciation of the absolute silence. Most people made an effort to fill the gaps with empty conversation. Grant took in deep breaths and kept his gaze on the horizon. Not once reaching for his phone.

She didn't have any idea how long they'd sat except for the sun blinking at the top of the farthest hill. "We need to head back to the Jeep before the sun completely sets."

Nodding, Grant took in one last sweeping gaze and pushed to his feet.

The walk down the hill was slow and steady. The way Grant walked slightly ahead and turned every so often to make sure she was still following, even lifted a hand to help her past a rock or root, made her smile. No point in mentioning to him that she'd run up and down this hillside every summer for so long that even in the dark she could find her way back to Hart House.

To her chagrin, the ride back flew by much faster than the trek out to Eagle Point. She pulled into an empty spot in front of Hart House. For the life of her, Violet couldn't figure out why time dragged during bad movies and awful company, but whizzed by when she was having a good time. Like now.

The man who had captured her sense of curiosity looked seriously more laid back and relaxed, like he belonged. So much so that she could almost forget he was here on a mission. Or a fool's errand.

"If you don't mind," his hand settled on the passenger door lever, "I'm going to run to the beach for a few minutes. I'd like to check my phone."

Or maybe that impression of a man more relaxed and laid back was just a figment of her imagination—wishful thinking. *Wishful?* What the heck would she be wishing for? That the playful man by the shore had truly learned to relax? Or that he…that he what?

"Earth to Violet." Grant waved his hand in front of her.

Immediately, her gaze shot from the lakefront ahead to the handsome man attached to the strong fingers spread open wide and waving at her. She shook away the crazy ideas ricocheting in the back of her mind. Not that his dimple-inducing smile was doing anything to help stop visions of her and him on the beach once again from taking over all rational thought.

"Is something wrong?" His smile slipped and a crinkled brow slid into place.

"No." Unless having brain freeze along with an inexplicable rush was wrong.

"Are you thinking about the studio? The flood? Or what's next?"

"Yes." Sure. That would work.

Grant chuckled and eased his hand back from the door handle. "Let's try something different. What if the new owners don't turn out to be all that bad?"

"Wouldn't that be nice." She pulled the key from the ignition and leaned back in her seat. "But I'm a banker's daughter and can do math. None of which ads up in my favor. If Mrs. Renfru sells—which seems highly likely—once the new owners trick out my former studio space, they'll have priced me out of the neighborhood. I'm not as worried about the apartment since that's under rent control."

"That could be a good thing if you don't want your landlady to sell. Most builders don't want to have their revenue prices locked."

"Isn't that just peachy." Stepping out of her car, she slammed the door harder than she should have. This was one time she wasn't even pretending to find the silver lining on this cloud. "Like it or not, it sounds more and more like that place will stay vacant and boarded up in perpetuity and I am about to get very up close and personal with the For Rent listings."

Arms resting on the roof of the Jeep, Grant leaned forward. "I know a lot of people in the landlord business. If you give me some of your criteria, I can put a word out."

"Thanks." Stepping back from the vehicle, she sucked in a good breath and blew out the bad. "Any help is always welcome."

"Okay." Pushing away from the vehicle, he nodded his head a bit too enthusiastically for a near total stranger who shouldn't care about her temporary rent crisis.

Funny, she'd spent more time with Grant the last two days than she had in weeks with the last two guys she'd dated, and yet she didn't know a whole lot about the man. She knew he was a developer, had a Navy grandfather, drove a drool-worthy Italian sports car, and liked ice cream. He could skim stones, appreciate a sunset, and send her heartbeat racing with a mere glance. Oh, and she shouldn't forget he was a good sport. She knew a boatload of men who wouldn't have sat in—or stretched in—a class like hers for all the money in Asia. Then again, maybe she knew more about him than she'd thought. Slipping her keys into her pocket, she backed away from the Jeep, still facing him. "I'll walk with you as far as your cabin, then over to mine."

He came to her side, easily matching his stride with hers. "I'm not stopping at the cabin, going straight to the reception area."

It took her a few moments to realize what he was talking about. The phone. "Understood. Will you be joining us for dinner tonight?"

"If that's an invitation, I'd love to."

Despite his need to be practically surgically attached to the phone, she was delighted he'd be joining them. "Tell me one thing?"

"Sure. I think." He bit back a smile.

"Did you work this hard even as a kid?"

"Let's say I did everything with gusto."

"Gusto?" What could possibly entail gusto at the age of ten? "Like?"

"My first tree fort." He chuckled. "Wasn't much of a fort and wasn't very high in the tree, but I did most of it myself and was pretty darn proud of it."

"Most?"

"About halfway through my grandfather came by to talk to my father. My dad was a great guy but he put the W in work."

"So it's genetic?"

"Maybe. A genetic work ethic could easily be involved, but I suspect it was more how I was raised."

Violet nodded. She wanted to hear more.

"Anyhow, my grandfather took one look at the fort, or what was supposed to be a fort and, rolling up his sleeve, he told me I'd done an excellent job, showed tremendous vision, and my skill set was admirable."

"But?"

"He didn't use that word but, he asked permission to help me finish as he rolled up. I thought it was the greatest thing in the world. That my busy grandfather would stop to help me build a fort."

"I bet that was great."

He nodded. "Even better, when my father arrived to meet with my grandfather, he rolled up his sleeves and chipped in."

"Oh, that's nice. I love my dad to death, but I don't think I could picture him building a tree fort."

"Honestly, until it happened, I wouldn't have thought so either. Anyhow, at that point, working side by side, I learned all about structural supports and joists and screw size and everything anyone might need to know about constructing a fort. Never forgot a single thing."

"And that's why you're in real estate?"

"Could be, and I'm good at what I do."

Oh, she didn't doubt that for a single minute. She may have been confused about a lot things, but she would wager big bucks at just how good he must be at what he does. "One more question?"

"Yes?"

"What's your favorite color?"

• • • •

How did they go from business to favorite color? Grant actually pondered if this was somehow a trick question. "Blue?"

"Are you asking me or telling me?" Violet grinned.

"Telling." How much trouble could he get into revealing his favorite color?

Her smile intact, Violet nodded. "Mine too."

More surprises. He would have expected something more girlish. Pink, purple, maybe daffodil yellow. Then he thought of a blue spring sky and thought how well it suited her.

The minute Grant had complied with her request and turned his cell phone off he'd anticipated the time when he'd be back at the shore and could turn it on. Even a time or two on the earlier walk along the shore, his mind wandered back to the silenced apparatus. But high up on the mountain, blanketed with peaceful silence and breathtaking views, the blasted phone hadn't crossed his mind even once.

By the time Violet had barely slipped the car into park, his mind once again snapped to attention and was running full speed ahead. Now silently approaching his cabin, he was torn between the adrenaline rush over getting back to what he did best, and leaving his lifeline to the real world turned off and soaking in this pristine rustic beauty. And wasn't that the dangdest thing? He'd vacationed from one end of the globe to the other. From the pink sandy beaches of Bermuda to this ski slopes of Chamonix. Not since his school days had enjoying the passing of time taken precedence over getting work done. Or maybe it was merely about spending more time with a woman who had sent his blood pounding with a simple high five. Perhaps when he returned to his cabin he'd look for a thermometer. A fever could explain a lot.

Slipping the contraption from his pocket, he pressed the button and listened to the musical tones as his only connection with the outside world came to life. Despite the flickering notifications of a long list of missed calls, Grant put on a smile and slid the thing back into his pocket. What would a few more minutes cut off from the world hurt?

They'd strolled past his cabin and Violet bit back a smile, pretending not to notice his deliberate avoidance of the very reason he'd returned to the lake shore—his phone.

"You know quite a lot about me from my hippie mother to my temperamental pipes. Tell me more about Grant Whitaker."

"Not much to tell. What you see is what you get."

"Oh, I bet there's a lot more behind those pressed pants and leather loafers."

"Nope. Ordinary kid. Played ball, any kind of ball, but loved baseball."

"Where you any good at it?"

"At baseball? Oh yeah. I could pitch at 75mph when I was still in junior high. By my senior year my fastball had dozens of universities and major league teams following my games, but I opted to go the straight academics route at Harvard like my dad."

"And your grandfather for his MBA."

He nodded. She paid attention. "Found I enjoyed playing Monopoly with real money and property more than baseball anyhow, so I guess I turned into a workaholic like the men before me."

"Ah, another point for genetics."

"Perhaps. Though both my father and my grandfather married fairly young. In that aspect, I'm not following in their footsteps. Which my grandfather does not waste an opportunity to remind me." Life and living had changed dramatically since his father's time, and even more so since his grandfather's time. The way Grant worked nearly twenty-four seven would not be fair to a wife, and he knew it. And as if trying to prove the point, his phone buzzed back to back to back before ringing loudly as it shook in his pocket.

He'd have preferred to ignore the calls, but a lot of people counted on him to do his job. His admin's name flashed across the screen. "Excuse me, I should take this."

Coming to a stop in front of the deep red door of her cabin, she smiled, nodded, and her gaze briefly locked with his before she disappeared behind the closing door. Blasted phone.

"Whitaker."

"I know you're busy, but I need to ask if you know anything about this new work order for the Paldao project?" Exasperation echoed in Madge's tone.

"I don't handle that kind of paperwork."

"I know that, but Joe has fallen out of touch again and the head of acquisitions brought this to me because it's not lining up with what he has."

"Did you ask the site supervisor?"

"Yeah. He doesn't know anything about it."

"Well, who signed off on it?"

"Joe."

"Then he's the one you have to talk to." Grant raked his fingers across the back of his neck. "Any idea what plumbing issue had him tied up and out of reach all day yesterday?"

Dead silence hung on the line. Madge was probably thinking the same thing he was. What did today's work order issue, yesterday's plumbing problems, and Joe's continued disappearance have to do with each other?

"All right. I'll keep digging. Forget I called and go enjoy the peace and quiet."

"Easier said than done."

"Which is exactly why you need to."

"Yes, mother."

"Good thing I happen to like your mother." Madge laughed, said goodbye and disconnected.

Grant's gaze drifted out across the lake then made its way back. Scanning the thick trees as far as he could see down the shoreline, he toyed with different options for all this land. The initial ideas that had danced around in his head didn't seem to be good enough anymore. A special place required a special idea.

Enjoy yourself, Madge had said. Memories of the mountaintop views pushed to the forefront of his mind. He had enjoyed himself very much today. Blowing out a heavy breath, he turned on his heel. Lights glowed in the distance from Hart House. Tucking his phone in his pocket, he hurried up the path. Whatever else he'd wanted to do this evening suddenly didn't seem nearly as inviting as a few hours at Hart House with the General and his very intriguing granddaughter.

CHAPTER TWELVE

Award winning. The words popped up every place Violet found the name F&W Development. Scrolling down, she skimmed yet another article. The diversity was just as impressive as the press photos. When she came across the massive shopping village in upstate New York, her heart sank. Surely he wasn't planning on putting something like that on Lawford Mountain? Not that it mattered. The plan was to build on Hart land and there was no way that would ever happen. Her grandfather would have to be on drugs to sell. But what if Grant didn't give up on Lawford and mowed down a mountainside to build a similar monstrosity? Once someone paves the way, others follow.

"Knock knock." Carrying a large dishtowel covered tray, Poppy nudged the door open. "When you didn't show up for supper, Lucy decided there couldn't possibly be enough food in your fridge to keep you from starving."

So engrossed in her research on Grant Whitaker, she'd completely lost track of time. "Sorry."

"Since when do yoga and computer research go together?" Poppy set the tray down on the nearby table. "Or are you hunting for a studio?"

Violet groaned aloud. "Don't remind me."

Leaning over her cousin, Poppy scanned the screen. "Impressive."

"This is only a fraction of what's out there." Violet clicked on another tab. "F&W Development has been revered for its high quality of standards, environmental friendliness, and ingenuity of design."

"Oh, look at this one." Poppy pointed to another caption with Grant looking terribly handsome in a sleek suit, shaking hands with a toothy grinning old man. "Golden handshake?"

Violet nodded. "Apparently it's known in the real estate community that despite the modern age of contract attorneys and breech litigation, a handshake deal with Grant Whitaker is as good as money in the bank."

A sharp whistle escaped from Poppy's lips. "Quite a compliment. And yet according to this, his firm is still one of the most profitable development companies in three states."

From all she'd read online, the all-business Mr. Whitaker was as much a throwback in time as Lawson's mountain community.

"Ooh, isn't that interesting." Poppy pulled up a chair and sat beside her cousin.

"What?"

"Look." Poppy pointed to another captioned photo on the left. "Talk about opposites attract."

Violet clicked on the photo. Where Grant was pressed and tailored, the same couldn't be said for his partner, Joseph Fiorello. Both men were in business casual but Grant looked like he'd just stepped off a sleek magazine cover and his partner looked more like he'd stumbled out of bed. His shirt might have been tucked in, but it remained puffy and loose, and sloppy. Grant had a hint of five o'clock shadow that made him look sexy and delectable. Joseph's dark shadow looked more like a man on the lamb from the law. Same could be said for their hair. Grant fell into the category of professionally groomed. While not quite a military cut, his hair definitely fell neatly above his collar. Unkempt was as nice a word as Violet could think of to describe the mop of hair falling every which way on Joseph.

The article below the photo wasn't any more flattering. From what Violet could glean reading between the lines, Joseph Fiorello might know how to build, but it was Grant's polish, business sense, and reputation that had made the company all they were. The duo reminded her a bit of her sixth grade history teacher's stories of the old Kennedy-Nixon debates. One man looked like the trustworthy guy next door and the other not so much.

Leaning back in her seat, Poppy continued to peruse the screen as Violet clicked from one article to the next. "I wonder what he's doing out here all by himself with a company like that to run?"

"You won't believe it." Pushing the mouse closer to her cousin, Violet stood to retrieve the dinner tray from the nearby table. "He thinks the General is going to sell him Hart Land."

"What?" If Poppy's eyes had shot open any wider they would have fallen out of their sockets.

"Relax." Violet waved at her cousin with one hand and skipping over Lucy's tuna casserole, stabbed at Lily's chocolate chip banana bread with the other. Watching her sugar intake was easy everywhere except around her cousin's baking. "You know that'll never happen."

Blowing out a deep sigh, Poppy pressed her lips together and nodded. "You're probably right."

"Probably?"

"Okay." Poppy smiled. "You're right. But why did he think our grandfather would ever sell?"

"Who knows? Something about a tip from his grandfather." Not till Violet slid a forkful of Lily's special banana bread into her mouth did she realize how hungry she was.

Poppy's wide eyed expression narrowed in confusion. "A tip? Where would anyone come up with something like that?"

Oddly enough, not till this second had Violet thought about it. "That is odd, isn't it?"

"I know he's only been here a couple of days, but surely by now he would have realized the tip is wrong. I mean, he and the General talked alone for almost an hour today. Wouldn't the property not being for sale have come up?"

Now that was something Violet didn't like. Of course it would have come up. *If* Grant had said anything. Had he? Her mind ran over any conversation they'd shared about his work and this property. "I think he mentioned something about surveying the possibilities. I don't think he mentioned having proposed the sale to the General yet."

"Well, that's good." Relief took over her youngest cousin's face. "It'll never happen. Nothing could make him sell."

Holding her next forkful of banana bread, her hand dropped back to the plate. "That's what I said!"

"So if we both know there's no chance it will ever happen, why do I feel like someone stole my lollipop?"

Yeah. That's what Violet wondered too.

• • • •

The minute Lucy had carried the tray out from the kitchen and announced it was for Violet, Grant almost jumped to his feet and offered to do room service delivery. All through dinner and most of the card game at hand, he'd been keeping one eye out for Violet. Well, maybe two. He'd felt like a kid in high school offered the perfect excuse to seek out and spend time alone with the prettiest girl in class and as deflated as an old balloon when Poppy took the tray.

Lady, or maybe it was Sarge, trotted over to him and nudged his hand in silent demand for a gentle stroke. The gesture was enough to draw Grant's attention back to the cards in his hand and away from thoughts of what Violet might be doing that was more important than the family dinner. It hadn't taken more than a couple of days and a handful of conversations to understand how important family time was to the yoga instructor.

"Old man Carter is probably rolling over in his grave." Ralph set a card down. "Hearts are trump."

The General shook his head and played a card. "That grandson of his was a spoiled brat when he was in diapers and things went downhill from there. A few years in the Corps would have straightened him out. Taught him respect."

"Now, Harold." In a nearby rocker, looking up from her project, Fiona Hart smiled. "Not everyone is meant for the military."

"Maybe not," the General eyed Grant's next play as he scooped up the trick, "but this rogue has caused his family and this community a whole lot of trouble, and hiding out in the south of France like the bloody Dauphine, he's practically getting off scot free."

Rogue? Dauphine? The turn of phrase shouldn't have surprised Grant. The General may be a jarhead, but there was no doubt he was a very well-educated jarhead.

"Well played." The older man nodded. "Always appreciate a man who understands the strategy of a card game."

"My grandfather taught me at a young age. I suspect it was his years at the Naval Academy that taught him the importance of thinking ahead and strategy. Whist and Bridge were his favorite card games."

"How about that." Ralph shuffled the cards. "Another Academy man."

"Another?" Grant asked.

Ralph handed the deck to the General to cut. "Yeah, just like—"

"Tell me, Grant." The General gathered his cards as Ralph dealt, cutting off his friend's comment. "What's your take on the Carter disaster?"

Quickly, Grant ran through the few articles he'd read on the Carter land crisis. Once upon a time the Carters had owned as much land as the Lawfords and Harts. Slowly, as each patriarch passed on, more and more of the land had been divvied out to the heirs. Brandon Carter III being the first born of the first born had inherited the bulk of Carter assets, including Carter industries. He'd also been a very naughty boy, using family land to dump toxic waste. "He should be tarred and feathered."

The General's grin spread across the width of his face. "Smart man."

"I'm all for earning a nice living." That car he'd fallen in love with at first sight cost a pretty penny to buy and then to maintain. "But there's a code every man should live by and *do no harm* is at the top of the list."

What he hadn't read up on lately was where the status of the situation was now. Last he'd read, the golden Carter boy had been living it up in the South of France as the General had mentioned, and rather than comply with environmental regulations and clean up, had chosen to simply shut down the remaining operations and abandon the land. "The shame of it is that he's probably making even more money manufacturing overseas, while the state is out of jobs."

"Not as many as you'd think." The General set his hand down. "His spoiled heirship—"

"Who?"

"Sorry." The General sighed. "Brandon the third. He'd cut US production so much by the time someone reported the late night trucking, there was hardly a local resident employed."

"It'll take the state forever to clean up that mess. If at all." Ralph shook his head.

"Old man Carter should have sold the land before letting that good for nothing grandson get his hands on it."

Bless you, Ralph. Just the lead in Grant needed. Not that he thought it possible the Hart granddaughters had anything in common with Brandon Carter III. All the girls he'd met were honorable and down to earth. He had a hard time imagining any of the remaining cousins as greedy land grabbers. "It's important to leave a legacy in the right hands."

"That it is," the General agreed.

"I bet keeping Hart Land running to a higher standard isn't easy."

Nodding his head, the General laid down a high trump card and slid the trick of four cards into his hand then stacked it neatly in a line with the other tricks. "It's definitely a lot of work, but certainly can't compare it to running the Marine Corps."

No. Grant supposed the problem of the US Marine Corps far exceeded the issues that would pop up on a daily basis at Hart Land. "Yet, keeping up with the cabins, the main house, the guests, the beach, and that wall—"

"Folks buying lakefront property nowadays aren't allowed to build out like that." A sly grin teased at the corners of the General's mouth.

"I would think not. I bet the lake zoning board is on you like white on rice for the upkeep and maintenance of that area."

"Like vultures waiting for it to collapse so they can reclaim the footage as theirs."

"Not at all surprised."

"So much of Hart Land is grandfathered in. From the septic that's too close to the creek for current zoning, to the sand we truck in every year after the winter washes most of it away."

"Sounds like it's more work than you let on?" Grant hoped he was baiting the trap well.

The General went silent organizing his cards. Grant had no idea if he was considering Grant's words or the hand he'd been dealt. "I suppose some would say that."

"Have you ever considered selling?"

"Every day." The General smiled and Grant's heart stood at attention. "And then I get out of bed and remember how much I love every inch of this place and everything that it means to this family."

Grant figured there was no time like the present to plant a seed of an idea in the old man's mind. "What if the right buyer came along? Someone who would honor this land as much as you have?"

"Never happen." Thelma shook her head and played a card. "This entire family bleeds Hart Land red white and blue."

"I don't think any of the girls would forgive you if you did." Fiona held the wooly haphazard pattern out in front of her.

"For what?" Poppy and Violet let the screen door slam behind them.

Louise laid a card down and scooped up the trick. "Selling this place."

"You're selling?" Poppy's eyes bugged open so large and round she'd have fit right in with a frightened flock of owls.

"Of course not!" The General scowled at the girls as if their words merited having their mouths washed out with soap. Or perhaps doing fifty one-armed pushups. Not a good sign.

Immediately, Violet's gaze darted in Grant's direction and he couldn't have felt worse if he'd kicked a puppy. "I believe we're talking *what if* scenarios," he clarified. "What if this land could be turned into one of the premier resorts of the east coast?"

"The east coast doesn't need anther premier resort. They dot the landscape from Maine to Miami already," Poppy said rather stiffly.

The General took the trick and once again neatly stacked it in a row beside him. "What was good enough for my grandfather and his grandfather before him is just fine for me."

"I can understand that. But which of your granddaughters is going to move in here and take over some day? Or will one of your daughters be doing that?"

The way the older man dragged his gaze away from his cards and peered over them at Grant, he wasn't sure if maybe this time he would be the one ordered to do fifty one-armed pushups.

From behind him, three voices chimed, "I will."

Joining Violet and Poppy, Cindy stepped into the card playing arena.

"I'm afraid, Mr. Whitaker," Poppy began. Uh oh, he'd gone from Grant to Mr. Whitaker. "You have underestimated the true value of

Hart Land."

To his chagrin, Poppy looked on the verge of tears. He didn't mind negotiating with a salty old Marine, but he wasn't prepared to do battle with a platoon of stunning and loyal granddaughters. From the way all the other eyes bore into him, he had certainly underestimated something. To his surprise, the only set of eyes not throwing daggers in his direction was a lovely shade of cobalt blue.

Violet failed to bite back a grin. Shrugging, she shook her head at him. "I told you. Never going to happen."

CHAPTER THIRTEEN

Adding a few extra minutes after her normal morning routine to remain on the floor in relaxing meditation with her legs raised on a hardback chair did wonders to ease the tension in her tired muscles. Too bad it did nothing to change the grim numbers showing up from one For Rent ad to the next. A groan escaped from deep down Violet's throat. Like it or not, she had to earn a living and nothing in her wanted to do so behind a desk, or for some trendy gym. She liked being her own boss. A lot. Too bad the Boston rental market didn't seem to agree with her.

The cost of anything even slightly usable as a studio near her apartment and clients had gone from pricey when she'd first started out, to astronomical. In order to find anything even remotely similar to her current studio, she'd have to move so far out to the fringes of the city that she might as well set up shop in the suburbs.

Fixing this situation was going to require a lot more than a hot shower, white noise, and deep breaths. Unraveling the towel from atop her head and tossing it onto the nearby chair, she scanned the pages one more time. Even though tempted to seek out more of her cousin's to-die-for chocolate chip banana bread to escape the dark side of real estate, she understood too well all that would accomplish would be to delay the inevitable. Decisions needed to be made and after scouring the options and tinkering most of the night with the numbers, she wasn't any closer to making up her mind than she'd been last night or again this morning. Maybe the banana bread wasn't such a bad idea. After all, bread was a staple at lunchtime and bananas were fruit. The chocolate chips were just the perks.

Dressed in her favorite yoga pants, she slogged up the hill to Hart House.

"We were expecting you for breakfast." Standing at the sink, Lucy waived a soapy hand at her. "I'm fixing grilled cheese and tomato soup for lunch. Hungry?"

Suddenly the yogurt she'd had for breakfast seemed so very long ago. "For your tomato soup? Always."

One by one, her cousins descended on Hart House. Working at the church, Poppy had more flexibility to join the family at lunchtime. Cindy could be hit or miss depending on if an animal crisis might be in progress at the veterinary clinic. Since lunch breaks were so short at the high school, the odds of Callie escaping to Hart House were usually pretty low. Today all the planets had aligned. Even Lily, on the brink of opening her own bakery, had settled into the Hart kitchen.

"I do love having so many of my girls together at one time." Fiona Hart waltzed into the room, going from granddaughter to granddaughter, bestowing a tender kiss on each woman's cheek.

"And where is our hunky guest today?" Cindy asked.

"Taking a walk with the General."

All sets of granddaughter's eyes zoomed in on Lucy.

"They left about an hour ago." Grams slid onto the seat at the round kitchen table, dragging her craft bag beside her.

Poppy's mouth dropped open and rounded eyes blinked back her concern. "That doesn't sound good. Could he be considering selling out?"

"Sell? Callie froze at the island, her voice increasing a notch in volume and indignation. "The General can't sell. Hart Land is part of the family.

Violet waved her hand. "Don't everyone get your panties in a wad over nothing."

"Nothing," several voices echoed loudly.

"How can you say that?" Poppy's lower lip came as close to a pout as Violet had seen since her cousin's childhood.

"Easy," she shrugged, "the universe and I are in perfect tune. The General is part of my universe. It's never going to happen."

Callie grabbed a cookie from a nearby dish. "You'd better be right."

"You'll see." Heather grinned. She had to be right.

"They should be back any minute. Flip these." Lucy handed the spatula over to Lily. "Make sure they don't turn too brown."

Without a word, Lily rolled her eyes, reminding everyone that they'd heard those exact words most of their childhood from the moment Lucy had deemed them old enough to man the grilled cheese griddle.

Lucy placed a well-packaged lunch into a basket. "I promised the folks in the Spruce cabin a hot picnic lunch. I'll be back in a jiffy."

Counting silverware from the drawer, Cindy leaned closer to the stove and lifting her chin, sniffed at the sizzling griddle. "Why is it grilled cheese never tastes this good when I make it at home?"

"Because Lucy won't tell us which is the secret cheese she adds!" Lily flipped a sandwich and scooped the next.

"If that woman was as good at matchmaking as she is at hiding her cheese supply, there wouldn't be a single person left in Lawford."

"Has anyone heard about any new matchmaking shenanigans?" Poppy gathered plates from the cupboard.

"Actually," Lily turned to face her sister, "no."

Poppy froze. "Okay, that's a bit scary. I mean, somehow I feel safer when I know someone else is in her sights."

"I know what you mean." Cindy closed the drawer. "I thought she might have brought Grant here for one of us, but as soon as we figured out there's nothing wrong with him, I knew it couldn't have had anything to do with Lucy."

"He does seem nice," Poppy agreed.

"Yes." Violet nodded, a grin spreading across her face.

"Ooh." Poppy stopped halfway out of the kitchen. "That sounds very… friendly."

Violet's gaze shot up.

"Oh." Cindy looked from Violet to her sisters and back. "That's way too big a grin for just friendly."

The rising heat in her cheeks was a dead giveaway that she was probably blushing like a rose. Not that she had anything more than an inexplicable electric moment to blame for it. "He is nice." Her cheeks grew warmer. "Very nice."

"Could it possibly be that Lucy finally got it right?" Lily slipped the last sandwich onto a plate.

"Nah." Cindy shook her head. "None of us knew she was coming up to visit. Not even Lucy."

"Did she?" Poppy asked Grams.

"What I think is that lunch is getting cold." Fiona Hart had sat so quietly hooking her rug, Violet almost forgot her grandmother was in the room. Setting her current project aside, Grams pushed to her feet. "And I'm sure your grandfather will be back any minute."

Violet's heart took off at double time. If the General was returning from his walk then Grant should be with him. Cindy was right. Friends didn't make her heart do somersaults for no reason. Carrying a stack of dishes into the dining room, she glanced through the window and spotted the duo down the hill. Her already dancing heart upped its tempo. By the time Grant followed the General in their direction, Violet's heart pounded more heavily against her ribs and there was no stopping the smile tugging at her cheeks. Oh brother was Cindy way more than right. Mr. Grant Whitaker had definitely charmed his way into her heart.

● ● ● ●

"You can see it, can't you?"

The vision for what to do with Hart Land was still fuzzy, but he knew enough to sell the idea. A few homes for full time residents but mostly a luxury resort. The New England mountains were filled with winter cabin resorts on a larger scale than Hart Land, but nothing the caliber Grant had in mind. "Most of it," he admitted.

"Sounds pretty complete to me." The General slowed his steps. His mind clearly at work. "In the summer when I was a boy the boats used to back up on the long pier by the One Stop. In those days, Katie's grandmother made her own candy and ice cream. Don't know that I've ever had ice cream that good anywhere else. Not even the Creamery in town."

The way Grant's stomach did a slow turn, he had a feeling whatever the General was thinking had a lot more to do with his proposal and not so much with ice cream. And not in a good way.

"Sometimes," the General stopped and spun about to face Grant, "progress isn't always the best approach."

"Or luxury?" He should have known any man that spent a lifetime of hard work and sacrifice wouldn't appreciate the fluff and puff, even buried in the pristine beauty of Mother Nature. Then again, maybe he'd known all along.

A grin spread easily across the old man's face as he picked up the pace back to the main house. "Knew you were a smart man."

"But..."

The General chuckled. "How long does it usually take you to get all of a plan? Not most. All."

This time Grant smothered a laugh. "The ideas come together pretty quickly during the research phase and is normally cemented once I'm done walking the acquisition."

"How many times have you walked this property?"

He'd yet to walk all of it, but he'd walked enough of it more than once. And pieces of the puzzle were still surprisingly missing, but he had to give this push everything he had. "I'd like to show you something if you'd allow me?"

Bushy white brows arched high on the General's forehead.

"I'll need to steal you for a long afternoon, but I think it will be worth it."

For a few long seconds Grant thought the old man would turn him down. An odd sense of relief mixed with disappointment filled him when the General nodded. "If you'll do the same for me."

"Deal." Grant stuck his hand out and the General quickly shook.

"Do you like grilled cheese?" The old man turned and marched up the stairs and inside of Hart house.

"Yes, sir."

"Good. You're going to love Lucy's."

No surprise there. So far everything he'd been fed had been worthy of a five star review. What Grant had to figure out and fast was the golden ticket to selling this deal to the General. The stumbling block to Grant's vision for this land came down to the hilltop bible. Mrs. Hart had said it his first day in the house, this wasn't property it was home. How to overcome that was the question. Shaking his head, he followed the General up the steps and into the house that everyone considered home. Happy chatter echoed inside. By the time he found a handful of the family hanging out in the kitchen, his heart dipped low in his chest at the realization he no longer had a reason to stay.

"Are you going to answer that?" Poppy waved at the vibrating phone on the counter between her and Violet.

"I'd rather not have anything spoil my lunch. I love Lucy's

grilled cheese."

The phone stopped and Poppy shook her head. "What if it had been notification from Publisher's Clearing House?"

Violet rolled her eyes at her cousin as the phone began dancing again on the countertop. Heaving a sigh, she snatched up the contraption. "Hello," she snapped. Her brows dipping into a perfect V. "Yes, hello Mrs. Renfru."

He moved closer to the reason he didn't want to leave Hart Land. At least not yet.

"Say that again?" She stuck a finger in one ear, looking skyward.

It took a minute for the V to unfold and her brows to arch. He wished she'd put the blasted thing on speaker.

"I see. You're sure?" Her lips curled upward at the edges. "And how long will that take?" The smile grew wider. "Sounds wonderful. Thank you for calling."

Grant inched closer. So close that if he took another step he'd walk through her.

Tossing her phone back onto the counter, Violet threw her arms in the air, squealed like a kid on Christmas morning, then spotting Grant, threw those same arms around him and squeezing tightly, squealed again.

It took a few seconds for him to remember they were in a public spot surrounded by gaping adults and unwrap arms that had too easily slid around her. Arms that felt surprisingly chilled at the loss of contact.

Long fingers eased their hold on his sides and Violet took a step back. Stunned eyes gazed up at him.

"You have news?" he managed to mutter.

"Yes." The earlier grin pulled at her cheeks slowly before blossoming into a full-blown smile. Spinning around, she faced her cousins and the exuberant energy of a few minutes ago bubbled forth again. "I don't have to move!"

"What?" Cindy hurried in from the dining room. "What's going on?"

"That was my landlord. She's accepted an offer on the building."

"Uh oh." Poppy frowned. "That doesn't sound like good news."

"But it is. Whoever's buying it will be updating the building, redoing the existing retail space and," her shoulders inched high in contained excitement, "honoring the existing rental rates."

"I thought you didn't have a lease?" the General asked.

"I don't." Violet's hands flipped palms up. "But that doesn't matter. She says they're honoring it and who am I to look a gift horse in the mouth?"

"How long will this take, dear?" Fiona Hart asked.

"That's the best part. My studio is first on the list. She says the paperwork has already been signed and the buyers are rushing the deal to close. They expect to begin rehabbing the building in ten days!"

Like a bunch of teens at camp, the cousins swooped in and did that group hugging dance thing that he'd seen young girls do more than once. Excitement bounced off the walls. His heart pumped rapidly against his ribcage. All he wanted was to join the group hug and dance around with Violet.

Frowning, the General shot a glance in Grant's direction. "Interesting turn of events."

"Mm," Grant mumbled.

"Rather poor business plan though. Don't you think?" The man stared pointedly at Grant. Could he possibly know?

"Depends on the buyer's motive."

"Mm," the General echoed his earlier response.

Grant smiled as innocently as possible. "Maybe someone's looking for a good tax deduction?"

"Mm," the General repeated, his gaze shifting to the group of women still squealing with joy. "Maybe."

Fiona Hart came to stand beside her husband. The man's arm instantly looped around his wife's waist and Grant's heart tightened when she casually laid her head against the older man's strong shoulders.

Shifting his attention from the couple beside him to the woman who flipped his every business plan upside down, Grant sucked in a deep breath and wondered for the first time ever if maybe he could emulate his dad and grandfather in more ways than good business sense.

CHAPTER FOURTEEN

None of yoga's deep breathing techniques could help slow Violet's racing heart. Between the good news from her landlady and the tingling nerve endings where Grant had wrapped his arms around her, she wasn't coming off cloud nine any time soon.

"That has to have been the best grilled cheese sandwich I have ever had." Grant set his napkin down on the table beside his empty plate, long fingers sliding away.

Those same fingers that reminded Violet of an artist, had been gently resting on her waist just a short while ago and she very much wished she could feel them against her once again.

Oblivious to the thoughts running through Violet's mind involving him, his fingers, and a whole lot of things she shouldn't be thinking about a man passing through on the way to his next big deal, Grant smiled at their longtime housekeeper. "The soup was the perfect accompaniment."

Lucy puffed up like a proud peacock. Anyone would think she'd never been complimented on her cooking before. "It's a family favorite."

"That's for sure," Cindy chimed in. "Though I've always had a hard time choosing between the tomato soup and Lucy's clam chowder."

Grant's brows cocked high on his forehead. "Clam chowder?"

"Yes," Lucy blushed like a virgin bride, "I'll have to make that before you leave us."

For a split second, Grant's expression looked as crestfallen as she felt at the thought of his leaving. How had she managed to become so ridiculously smitten with a near stranger and so quickly?

"So what happens now?" Lily asked.

"Huh?" Violet blinked. With Grant? Not much. He was leaving. Soon.

"With the new owner," Lily clarified.

"Oh." Violet really was letting her mind run away with her. "I guess I wait. At least that's what my landlady said."

"You don't think the new buyers will change their mind, do you?" Poppy asked.

"Oh, I hope not."

"They won't." Grant shook his head, then froze.

"Do you know something the rest of us don't?" Violet asked.

The way Grant's eyes widened at her little tease, for a moment Violet wondered if he really did know something she didn't know.

Narrowing her gaze, she considered that last thought. "Did you send one of your clients her way?"

The man's eyes grew momentarily wider before he relaxed, smiled and shook his head. "No. Didn't connect a client with your landlady."

"But you are pretty sure the sale is going to go through?"

He shrugged. "Few developers throw around letters of intent for the heck of it."

"Did I mention a letter of intent?" She really wasn't sure if she had.

Those big twinkling eyes grew round again. "Did they give her an actual sales contract?"

"Oh. I don't know." Now she felt silly. Of course he wouldn't know any more than she did. "All Mrs. Renfru mentioned was that she'd received a very good offer and that the new sellers were anxious to fix the place up. Apparently they really like the idea of the yoga studio and how it will appeal to the demographic they'd be going after."

"I suppose that does make sense." Cindy pushed away from the table. "Everyone is so self conscious of lifestyle lately. Organic foods. Hormone free products. No sugar. Exercise. A balanced life. Makes perfect sense."

"Well, whatever the reason," Violet smiled at her cousin, "I'm thrilled."

"You weren't looking too happy with the For Rent ads anyhow." Poppy laughed.

"No." Violet brushed away the tightening in her gut that snuck up on her every time the idea of real estate shopping came up. "Can't say that I was."

Grams pushed to her feet. "Well, I'm delighted with any prospect that keeps you here at the lake a little longer."

"Here, here," the General agreed, rubbing his hands together. "What's on the agenda for this afternoon?"

Up until a short while ago, the only thing on Violet's schedule had been to hunt for a new studio home. Now she wasn't so sure.

"I've got to head back to the clinic." Cindy slung her purse over her shoulder and sighed. "We're trying to care for a nest of baby birds that got knocked over in last week's storm."

Poppy shoved her chair against the table and followed her sister. "Do you need some help?"

"Yes." Cindy spun around. "They require hand feeding so often. What we really need is a facility set up for the care of injured wildlife. I do my best but…"

"We know you do, dear." Grams let her hand rest gently on her granddaughter's arm. "You do better than most."

The General's brows knit together. His lips pressed tightly closed, he stared at his granddaughters as they exited the room with their grandmother.

"Whatya thinking, General?" Violet sidled up by the old man.

"Folks get real comfortable with the status quo."

Violet nodded.

"I think," he bobbed his head and began walking, "it's time this mountain shook up the status quo. Change isn't always easy, but when it's time, it's time."

Before Violet could fully process a response, the General had caught up with his wife and left Violet rooted to the floor, her mind racing. Just how much *change* was her grandfather planning to make?

● ● ● ●

Grant hung back as everyone scurried off to their day jobs. Poppy back to the church, Lily to her bakery project, and Cindy to the veterinary clinic. Here at Hart House, Lucy headed to the kitchen, the General with his faithful retrievers at either side of him closed the door to his office behind him, and Mrs. Hart sank into to her favorite chair and most recent project.

"What exactly is she making?" he asked.

The only person not running off, Violet stood near the front doorway staring after her grandfather. "Excuse me?"

"Your grandmother. She's been working on what I thought was a rug since I got here, but she doesn't seem to be making any progress. Could it be something else?"

Violet tore her gaze away from her grandfather's office door. For the first time since meeting her, he clearly detected worry in her eyes. Not even when she was dealing with the unknown fate of her business did she have such a dark shadow in her eyes.

"Is something wrong?" He had to resist the urge to ease forward, brush a loose strand of hair from her face and maybe let his fingers linger down her cheek. Man, when did he get it so bad?

Literally shaking her head, she seemed to brush off whatever had concerned her and lifted her gaze to meet his. "I'm sorry. What?"

Losing himself in those deep soulful eyes, his mind went totally blank.

"Grant? What did you say?"

"Oh." He looked away, spotted Mrs. Hart, remembered the thread of conversation, and just as quickly, could have cared less about the project. "Are you still worried about the building, because I can assure you the deal is legit."

She blinked, smiled, then frowned so quickly if he'd blinked he would have missed most of the thoughts rushing through that pretty head. "I thought you didn't have anything to do with the new buyers."

Everything in him told him that if he wanted this relationship to go any further—and right now he didn't even have the right to call what little they had a friendship, never mind a relationship—he needed to be totally honest but not spill his guts. "What I said was that I did not bring a client of mine to your landlady."

Her lips pressed tightly together and her chin jetted out. He felt like a schoolboy in front of the principal. "I heard your handshake and your word are as good as a written contract."

He nodded. "I guess I'm more old-fashioned about some things."

"You're more old-fashioned about a lot of things, but that's beside the point. You didn't get a reputation like that by being a liar."

"That's because I don't lie." Though he did choose his words very carefully more often than not.

"You look awfully serious, dear." Mrs. Hart glanced up from her project. Her timing couldn't have been any better. If it wouldn't look absolutely ridiculous, he'd stroll over and kiss the woman.

"Just thinking a few things out, Grams." Violet strolled over to the older woman and lifted a corner of the heavy piece. "What exactly is this?"

Fiona Hart blew out a deep sigh. "It's supposed to be a small rug for the kitchen. I thought a pretty floral bouquet would be lovely for spring."

"Sounds like a great idea."

"Except," she let her hands fall on the patterned netting thing, "it doesn't look anything like I expected."

Both Grant and Violet inched closer. For the first time, Grant took a good look at the thing she kept stabbing and the sections of work already covered with colored strips of yarn. For one thing, the yarn sections were inconsistent. Some were thick and plush others were almost balding. Also, some of the yarn was longer than others, as if the thing needed a good barber.

"What did you expect?" Violet asked.

Fiona looked down at the work in progress. "I suppose for the flower garden to look like flowers."

Taking a closer look, he realized the sweet lady was indeed having a hard time staying within the lines. Her purples seemed to be bleeding into her yellows and a few of the petals had taken on rather awkward shapes.

"I also suppose," this time Fiona Hart smiled, "I should be happy it's still an even rectangle."

For reasons that clearly only Violet and her grandmother understood, Violet burst into laughter, making the other woman grin even wider. Then Violet bent over and kissed her grandmother on the forehead. "Thanks, Grams, for always reminding me to keep things in perspective."

"Life is a tapestry. Sometimes we can't see the final picture until the key stitches are finished."

"Maybe that's the case with your rug?"

Fiona Hart shook her head and smiled. "Somehow, I don't think so."

Intently watching the interaction between Violet and her grandmother, Grant was overcome with an unexpected need to visit his own grandmother. So much so, he almost didn't realize the cell phone in his pocket vibrated from an incoming call. He really wished he understood the rhyme or reason to why every once in a blue moon the blasted thing actually worked. Turning his back to the woman and taking a step away, he fished the phone from his pocket. "Hello."

"Mr. Whitaker."

"Yes."

"Jim Kelly here."

The Paldao foreman. Grant had limited interaction with the construction sites, but still he knew every foreman and site supervisor, even a good number of the construction crews, well enough to inquire about their lives and family. Something his grandfather had taught him since he was out of diapers. Every human being deserves basic respect. "Hi Jim. This is a surprise." Unless this had something to do with the work orders Madge didn't understand.

"Sorry to bother you, but I can't get a hold of Mr. Fiorello."

"What's up?" He took a few steps closer to the doorway and hoped the call didn't drop.

"I know he's been dealing with the Pex pipe ruptures at the Farmington Mall."

"What?" How had he not heard about this? Farmington Mall was almost ready to turn over. And how the hell did the PEX pipe rupture? That piping was the best invention since the wheel.

"I think we may have a similar problem coming on my site."

Grant pinched the bridge of his nose. Jim would be taking over soon as site supervisor for the last phase of the Paldao condominium complex across the state. "What exactly have you found?"

"I got to thinking about the weakest point in the piping."

Even though Jim couldn't see him, Grant nodded.

"It would make sense it's the brass fittings that connect the pipes."

Grant nodded again.

"I know it sounds silly, but when I came up with the brass fittings, the hairs on the back of my neck stood up. I decided it was worth checking out on my site."

The hairs on Grant's neck were at attention also.

"Sure enough. Our leftover supplies. Every fitting had defective thread tapping, with cracks at four spacings of the thread tapper."

Grant wasn't an engineer or a plumber but he knew whatever the young man had just said to him was not good. "And you haven't told Joe?"

"I can't get a hold of him. Been calling all day. If the problem is what I think it is, he's going to have to check every connector on every pipe."

Any layman would be able to grasp the severity of those last words. And the cost.

"And Mr. Whitaker?"

"Yeah?"

"These aren't our regular fittings."

"What do you mean?"

"We've always bought ours from the same local supplier for as long as I've worked for F&W. When I took one by to show them, a machinist said it wasn't one of theirs. He confirmed that in his view, the thread tapper was rotating at too fast a rate, adding that he thought the brass to be substandard quality and likely had too much zinc in the mix, compared to copper. Insists it wasn't one of theirs."

Oh hell. "Call Larry and see if he has any info, then call the office. Explain to Madge what you just told me. If the two of you can't reach Joe by morning, go ahead and do a re-inspect of every connector joint in the place. I'd rather lose time and money now then have the damn thing turn into a water show worthy of Niagara Falls."

Maybe Violet was right. At this moment he certainly agreed peace and quiet was king and cell phone reception was highly over-rated.

CHAPTER FIFTEEN

"Are you all right?" Harold Hart tapped one last word on his keyboard and leaned back into the warmth of his wife's hand squeezing his shoulder. "There's so much to do."

"You've said that before, but you're doing much better, everything will work out."

"Still, I might have been a little shortsighted." He didn't need to look up to know his wife's eyes were open wide. Not in surprise but more in a loving look of disagreement. She'd been his best cheerleader for so long, he couldn't remember his life before her, and frankly, shortsighted was rarely a word in his vocabulary.

The same warm fingers pressing gently on his shoulder lifted with a flourish to press against his forehead in mock measurement of his body temperature. "Just checking." She leaned forward and kissed his cheek. "Wouldn't want you having a relapse."

With one quick motion, he tugged her around onto his lap, much the way he'd done whenever he was fortunate enough to come home to his family.

Under her breath, Fiona chuckled, her face bright and smiling. "Oh, you are feeling better."

He let his lips settle sweetly against hers for a tender moment in time. "I am now."

"So now what?" Her fingers linked with his.

"Cindy's right." He sighed. "It's time to stop kicking the can around and take care of mountain business."

Snapping her spine straight, Fiona grinned and gave a mock salute. "And here we go again!"

• • • •

Her grandfather couldn't actually be considering selling. Violet wrapped her arms around herself and brushed off a chill. Even her grandmother had seen the shift in the General's attitude over lunch. Grams rarely bothered her husband when he was playing on his computer or chatting with his friends, but when she'd set her rug aside to stretch, she'd stretched all the way to the General's office and closed the door behind her.

So focused on what her grandparents were talking about behind closed doors, Violet didn't notice when Grant disconnected his call and walked up beside her.

"Sorry, I had to take that." He shook his head. "I don't understand how everyone doesn't go crazy not knowing when this phone will or won't work."

"Most of the time we just use the landline." She shrugged. "Besides, when any of us are up here, we don't really care about staying connected to the outside world." A shiver skittered up her arms. She didn't even want to think about losing the lake. This place had been as much a part of her for her entire life as her arm or leg.

The office door squeaked open, and holding his wife's hand, General Harold Hart came out of the room smiling. "Oh good." He looked to Grant. "You still up for that ride you promised me?"

Grant nodded and fell into step behind the General.

Not waiting for an invitation, Violet hurried behind them. "Where are we going?"

"To fix the mountain." As if still a much younger man, her grandfather stomped down the steps and trotted over to his vehicle.

Violet had to quicken her pace to keep up.

Thanks to his longer legs, Grant beat her to the car and held the passenger front door open for her.

A polite round of thank you and your welcome was exchanged as the General buckled himself in and started the Jeep. Violet was pretty sure whatever had her grandfather in such a hurry, to him, it was enough that if either of them had not climbed in quickly, the old man would have left without them.

"I don't suppose you want to explain more clearly where we're going?" Violet clipped her seat belt into place.

"I told you. Fix the mountain."

"Of course," Violet mumbled. She didn't even know what was

broken with the darn thing never mind how he was planning to fix it. "I don't suppose you'd care to share exactly what it is we're fixing?"

Not until the car was off Hart property and on the main road out of town, with his gaze fixed in the rearview mirror on Grant, did the General respond. "You work with a lot of construction companies in the state, correct?"

"Yes sir."

"And you work with a large pool of investors for different projects. Also correct?"

"That's an accurate statement."

"You also must know other developers who work in this part of the country?"

This time Grant merely nodded.

"And if a particular project is not suited to your company, you would know which investor and construction company would be better suited to each other. Wouldn't you?"

Grant bobbed his head. "A fair assumption."

"Good." The General waved his arm from Violet in the passenger seat, across the dashboard to his left. "This mountain is one of the most beautiful places on the planet. I should know, I've traversed most of it."

"I won't argue with you. I agree. Only a few hours outside of the major metropolitan area and a person could easily believe they'd stepped back in time. No pollution. No traffic jams. Friendly neighbors. Checker games in the barber shop on Main Street." Grant shook his head and sighed. "Definitely someplace special."

"Glad you agree." The General turned off the main southbound drag and onto the road that would take them across the lake. "What do you know about government clean ups?"

"Of what?" Grant asked. Though Violet didn't know why. If she'd figured it out, surely he had to know where her grandfather was going with this.

"Toxic waste."

Grant nodded, and Violet could see in his eyes that recognition had dawned. "I presume you're speaking of the old Carter factory?"

"Exactly. I know what I think of the whole situation, but I'd like to have your first-hand opinion. It's time this community stops gossiping about the family genetics and began putting things to right. If anyone can comprehend the complexity of government red tape, I'd be your man."

Grant chuckled softly. "Everything in triplicate, sir?"

"And then some." The General glanced at the rearview mirror and Grant. "Have you done any projects that required cleanup?"

"Not with F&W, but yes."

"What has to happen to make it worth a company's while?"

"Depends. But usually these things take time, and like the old saying goes, time is money. Most developers can't waste any of either."

Her grandfather pressed his lips tightly together and nodded. For the next little while, no one said much of anything, but she knew Grant was taking in every inch of the scenery along the side of the road. She didn't need to be a mind reader to know he was probably doing the math. What she wasn't sure of was if it had something to do with this impromptu country drive or Hart land.

"And we're here." The General turned into an open gateway.

Violet expected to find a hallowed estate at the end of the long driveway, instead a rather sad looking structure stared back at them.

Silently, they each exited the car. Grant took in everything in the world around him. "This is the Carter place?"

"It is." The General stood at what Violet had learned along time ago as parade rest. The man was waiting for Grant to finish his assessment.

As well as Violet knew her grandfather, the thing she didn't know was what the General expected from all this. From the way he held himself, the one thing she'd bet on was that her grandfather knew what was coming next. Too bad she didn't have a clue.

• • • •

It might have taken a moment longer than it should have, but Grant finally pieced together what the General meant by fix his mountain. The old man wanted someone to come in and do the caliber of clean up that would exceed anything the government could manage in a fraction of the time.

In an effort to ease the growing tension, he ran his hand forcefully to and fro across the back of his neck. "Exactly how much do you know?"

"His spoiled heirship hightailed it out of here almost two years ago. Though he'd clearly been prepping for a while, even before the regulators came knocking on his door."

Grant nodded. He'd gleaned pretty much the same, but had only skimmed the article he'd stumbled across. "Do you know where the dumping was happening?"

"Assuming he wasn't doing this behind everyone's backs since he took over, yes. A map was printed in the local paper, breaking the story."

Now he remembered. "The chemicals in the barrels they found were identified mostly by labels."

"Correct."

"Have samples already been packaged and sent to a lab for analysis?" It had been years since Grant had anything to do with toxic cleanup, but he remembered more than he thought.

"Some."

"But not all." His one hand scrubbed at the back of his neck. "Do you think this was going on before his heirship took over?"

A slow grin eased its way across the General's face. Apparently Grant had scored a few brownie points with the use of the heirship title. "No way. His daddy and granddaddy before him were as honest and upright as Abe Lincoln and a California Redwood."

"Okay. The process for cleaning up a hazardous waste site is long and complicated. The longer this site has been sitting, the more serious the soil and water table contamination, but the only way to know for sure is with testing. A lot of testing."

The General merely nodded. "I think, if we can get a reputable developer involved, the towns around here might be willing to kick in a little something to help."

Grant didn't have the nerve to tell the General that even if there was very slight contamination, the towns' *kick in* would have to be way more than little.

"There's an awful lot of land up here by the main buildings that shouldn't be affected at all, but no one wants to buy near that mess down the hill. If clean up were done right…" He lingered, looking around. "This could make a great facility for care and preservation of wildlife."

That was a tall order, but now Grant understood where the old man was coming from. "I suppose I could look into things. Put out a few feelers."

Slapping his hands together loudly and rubbing them hard enough to spark a fire, the General's grin spread even wider. "That's all I could ask for."

"That would be great. I just can't imagine how all these neighbors feel. So many people live near here." Violet shuddered and Grant resisted the urge to wrap an arm around her shoulders and warm the chill away.

How many days had he been here that he felt such a strong pull to not only Violet but the whole blasted mountain. The lake, Main Street, the Hart house, the General and his family, heck even Lucy the cook had easily coaxed him out of his Mediterranean heart healthy dietary habits. And Lily was bound and determined to single handedly clog all his arteries with all those real butter heavy baked goods of hers, especially the banana bread. But Violet was the true catalyst. He honestly didn't care what the cost of a building might be or the price tag of a hazardous waste cleanup. What seemed to matter most to him was making her smile. If he didn't finish up his business, that smile might be his most expensive habit yet.

CHAPTER SIXTEEN

"Yes, ma'am." After playing cards all night with friends and guests, Violet had opted to sleep in this morning. Hungry, she had to choose between the balance of life and reality she got from her morning yoga routine, or raiding the Hart House fridge. Hunger had won. On her way to snoop through Lucy's kitchen, her landlady called. Lifting her head to the warm sun, Violet could feel the heat deep in her bones. One of the drawbacks of living in the heart of Boston was the lack of sunshine thanks to the tall buildings.

"I have wonderful news for you. We're signing the papers Monday afternoon, but the buyer's project manager would like to meet with you first thing that morning to nail down the plans."

"So soon?" She'd hoped the sale would actually go through, and that the buyer would keep his word, but she hadn't expected anything this fast.

"Yes, isn't it wonderful?" The enthusiasm in the old woman's voice matched the way Violet felt.

"Do you know what time?"

"No, I expect they're going to call you directly since the man I spoke with asked for your number. I hope you don't mind that I gave it to him?"

"No, of course not. I look forward to hearing from him. And thank you."

"Don't thank me dear, thank whoever it is buying this old building."

A few more words and Violet slid her phone into her pocket, sucked in one more breath of fresh lake air deep in her lungs and took the front porch steps two at a time. With a single phone call, she'd gone from hungry to ravished and had a strong yearning for some of her cousin Lily's banana bread.

"Well don't you look chipper this morning?" Her grandmother

wiped her hands on a nearby towel and spun around to hug Violet.

"I got good news."

"About the apartment?" Her grandmother's words tumbled over Lucy's comment, "You've got a date?"

Violet did her best not to roll her eyes at the housekeeper. "I'm meeting with the new owner's construction people on Monday morning."

"Oh, that is good news."

"Where is everyone?" Violet stepped out of her grandmother's embrace and glanced around the large kitchen.

Grams held back a knowing grin. "Your grandfather left early for Floyd's. A few of the cabin guests checked out first thing."

"Checked out?" Violet's heart shot up to her throat. Grant hadn't said a word about checking out. Though he had left the card game after a couple of hours when a call made it to his phone.

Her grandmother's eyes twinkled with amusement. "Grant said he was going to try and get some work done. I suspect he'll be by the lake."

Relief washed over her in a wave so strong that she almost stumbled back into the nearest chair. She hadn't expected the high level of distress at the thought of Grant leaving, nor the relief at knowing she still had more time with him.

"Your timing is perfect." Lucy slid a clean frying pan into the cupboard. "I was just going to call you."

"Yes," her grandmother said, "I've decided to give my leftover craft supplies to the church bazaar. We were just about to head up to the attic and see if we could find anything else to donate."

Heaven knew her grandmother had a stash of unused crafting supplies to stock a major chain store. The woman had flittered from one thing to another, but had yet to find something that liked her as much as she liked it.

Lucy shut the cabinet door, removed the oversized apron, and leaving it on a nearby hook, led the three women up to the third floor. Unlocking the narrow door that led to the attic, she stepped aside for Violet and her grandmother to start up.

"Oh my." Her grandmother waved an arm across her face, brushing aside some cobwebs. "I guess it's been a while since I've been up here."

"You and me both." Lucy fisted her hands on her waist and glanced around. "Do you want to start with the back or the boxes here in front?"

Violet whizzed past the two women. "This place isn't as creepy as I remember."

"Creepy?" Grams asked.

"Yeah." Violet opened the old chest her cousins and her had used the contents of to play dress up. "Cindy and Iris were braver than me. They loved rummaging through the old stuff and making up games. I hadn't joined the fun until I'd outgrown my fear of the Boogeyman."

Grams chuckled. "What have you got there?"

"Clothes. We'd dress up and then pretend we were ghosts haunting the attic. Sometimes we'd sneak downstairs."

"And scare the bejeesus out of people." Lucy smiled. "I remember it well."

"Don't tell me you believe in ghosts?" Grams asked.

Lucy shook her head and shifted a box in front of her. "I just didn't expect anyone to be popping out of the closets."

"On behalf of my entire generation of Hart descendants," Violet stood and curtseyed, "I apologize."

Lucy bit back a smile and forced a gruff, "Apology accepted."

"I don't remember this." Violet made her way to a back corner by a window.

Grams ran a hand across the dusty dresser then reached over and nudged the cradle. "This has been in the family for as long as your grandfather can remember. He rocked in this as did your mom and aunts. I always thought we'd bring it back down when the next generation arrives."

"It's beautiful. They don't make furniture like this anymore."

"China," Lucy huffed. "With staples."

"There are still some craftsmen around." Her grandmother walked over to an enormous stand up steamer trunk. "I don't remember what's in here."

"More clothes," Violet answered, then shrugged. "What can I say, we played a lot."

"I suppose we should donate these to the school's theater department. I doubt they're ever coming back in style." Grams ran her fingers through the hanging garments and closed the trunk.

"Oh look." Lucy opened a nearby box. "Christmas decorations. We could donate these, don't you think?"

Grams looked into the box and slowly shook her head. "What if the girls want some family mementos for their own homes?"

One brow raised higher than the other, Lucy dipped her chin to glare at Grams. "Is this going to happen with the entire attic?"

"Well, I did say we could donate the old clothes to the high school theater department."

"That you did." Lucy nodded and opened another box and a similar conversation ensued.

By the time an hour or so had passed and a slew of boxes had been opened and examined, Violet knew that her grandmother wasn't going to find it in her heart to part with any of the treasures in the attic. "I don't know about any of you, but my stomach is rumbling. Why don't we take the crafting supplies downstairs and bring up some bags for the theater donation?"

"Good idea." Dressed in a bright pink floral blouse over a pale blue scarf skirt, Grams stretched left and right creating a billowing picture. She really was beautiful at any age.

"I'm really feeling hungry now." Violet grabbed one of the bigger boxes and started down the stairs. At the bottom, juggling the box on one hip, she turned the knob and slammed into the door. "What the…"

Behind her, Grams held a smaller box. "What's the matter, dear?"

"The door won't open." She tried again. Nothing.

"Is it stuck?" Lucy called from the top of the stairs. "Maybe we should call the fire department."

"Don't be silly. Let me try." Grams put her box on the step and shimmied around Violet. The door rattled but didn't budge. "Oh my."

"Now should I call the fire department?" Lucy asked.

"No!" both Grams and Violet echoed.

"Maybe I can call out to someone from the window?" Violet looked to her grandmother. "It's a nice day. Maybe George will hear us?"

Lucy shook her head and marched up the stairs, letting Grams and Violet pass her. "He's in town picking up supplies."

Violet didn't let that slow her plan down. Much. She huffed, shoving at a wooden pane. "How long has it been since these windows were opened?"

"Since no one spends any real time up here," Grams hefted a shoulder, "I'm going to guess decades may be too little."

"Argh," Violet grumbled, trying a second and third window.

"I have my phone." Lucy held it up. "Fire department is only a call away."

Violet didn't bother to respond and marched down the steps, trying the knob again.

"I'm sure any one of Cole's strong firemen friends could get it open," Lucy tried again.

"Actually," Violet twisted the knob, "I don't think it's stuck. I think it's locked."

"Locked?" Grams asked.

Through a haze of confusion, things were starting to make sense to Violet. Especially Lucy's eagerness to call the fire department. "Lucy…"

The woman had the audacity to smile at Violet with the innocence of a newborn babe. *Not likely.* "Yes?"

"Did you lock the door?"

"Now why would I do that?" Lucy's expression didn't falter.

"Lucy?" Grams asked.

"Honestly," Lucy waved her arms and then slid her hands into her dress pockets, "I didn't. Oops." Drawing both hands out simultaneously, one gripped the skeleton key that had been used to open the door in the first place. "I must have done it without thinking."

Right. Without thinking. Violet should probably have been happy the windows didn't open or Lucy might have thrown the dang thing out the window until they had no choice but to call the fire department for real. Why couldn't Cole's buddies have all been happily married instead of good looking and single? Or better yet, if Lucy was going to lock anyone in the attic, why couldn't it have been

Violet and Grant?

• • • •

"Where the heck have you been?" Grant paced along the section of land the Harts referred to as the Point.

"I told you, I was resolving a problem." Joe sounded frustrated, or tired, or maybe both. "I don't understand why you and Madge are so bent out of shape over a little lack of communication."

"Considering that cell phone of yours is one step shy of surgically attached to you, it shouldn't come as a surprise that not being able to reach you could be alarming."

"Yes, so Madge explained." Joe sighed and Grant could almost see the man rubbing the tension headache away. "I promise the next time my phone falls into a bucket of water and dies I will send smoke signals if I have to, but I'll let you and Madge know. Is that enough?"

"It is but—" The buzzing of Joe's phone could be heard.

"Ah hell, I have to take that. Just relax and enjoy the lake and bring back a sales contract."

"Yes. About that—" The phone buzzed again.

"I really have to go. Will touch base in a few days." And just like that the call disconnected.

What the heck was going on? Everything seemed to be upside down on the jobsites and if Grant didn't know better he might think Joe was avoiding him. At least the rest of his morning had been more than productive. Though he still wished he didn't have to hang out in a lounge chair in order to have access to internet. His research on the Carter property was both intriguing and distressing.

"You look like someone stole your puppy." Violet approached, giving his heart a kick.

"Not exactly." He slid his phone into his pocket. Maybe he'd accomplished enough for one day.

"Well," she sidled up beside him, "at least no one locked you in the attic."

"What?" Instinctively his head turned to the main house and back.

On a heavy sigh, Violet dropped to the ground and sat cross

legged. "Lucy."

"Does Lucy make a habit of locking you in the attic?" Not knowing what else to do, he dropped to the ground beside her. Once again thankful she'd made him buy jeans.

"No. Though she did lock a couple in the shed once."

Grant could feel his forehead folding in confusion.

"Did I ever mention that Lucy considers herself a gifted matchmaker? A modern day Dolly Levy?"

"No, but I did notice she hums the song a lot. Any connection?"

Violet nodded. "It's her ringtone too. Let's just say she's capable of extremes if she thinks two people would be good for each other."

"How extreme?" Grant held his hand up. "Never mind, you said something about locking two people in a shed."

"Or burning a house down."

"What?"

Violet shook her head. "I shouldn't have said that. In all fairness, it wasn't a real fire. She just lit the wood and forgot to open the flue."

"Should I ask why?"

"She seems to have taken a fancy to firemen." Violet straightened her legs, made circles with her ankles to the left, then to the right before leaning back on her elbows, stretching her neck side to side and finally tilting her up to the sun. Lord, from head to toe she looked amazing. "I think the reason she locked us in the attic was to have an excuse to call the fire department. Not sure which one she has her eye on, but I suspect any single and fit fireman would do."

For reasons he couldn't begin to explain, Grant wanted to go fight someone over this and didn't have a clue who. Certainly not a nice lady like Lucy.

"Anyhow," she tipped her head back toward him, "what's got you looking so down?"

"Business. Trying to tie up a few deals." He stretched out beside her. "Did a little research on the Carter thing."

"Really?" She sprang up, leaning over him. "And it's not good?"

"Well, it's complicated."

She stared, waiting for more.

"If—and that's a big if—the contamination hasn't reached the water tables, there's a chance clean up could happen and return to safety levels soon enough to be worth buying and holding the property."

"But that's good news, right?"

"Maybe." Oh, how he wished she'd just move a few inches closer. She looked so blasted kissable. How long had it been since being around a woman made him feel like a crushing, hormonal teen? He weaved his fingers with hers and swallowed hard when her hand closed around his and she smiled. "I know I'm changing the subject, and this may sound a bit stupid, but can I kiss you?"

Her eyes blinked, the smile slipped, and her head nodded ever so slightly he could have easily missed it if he wasn't so focused on her mouth. Soft lips met his, her weight pressing against him as she leaned into the kiss. His heart pounded so hard and fast she had to feel it. In the distance he heard a car door slam but let the kiss linger. Another door slammed and this time a wolf whistle snatched his attention. Turning to look, he caught a glimpse of a hulking guy elbowing the slimmer guy beside him who must have done the whistling.

Like an over-wound spring, Violet jumped to her feet and Grant could have kicked himself for kissing her out in public like that. What if the General had been the one to see them? "Sorry," he whispered.

"Nothing to be sorry about," she replied softly, smoothing out her skirt.

"Violet?" the big voice called out, while the other guy headed to the main house.

The way her eyes narrowed then widened told him that she recognized the hulking figure now walking in their direction. The smile that crossed her face told Grant he wasn't very happy about it.

"That is you."

"Payton. What brings you here? Are Cole and Lily coming too?"

Mr. Hulk wrapped his beefy hands around her waist and tugged her into a warm embrace and Grant bit down on his back teeth. "Nah, Lucy called."

Violet rolled her eyes. "What for?"

"A donation of stuffed toys."

"Toys?"

"Yeah, for handing out to kids after car accidents or a house fire.

Always glad to pick up a donation. If we can't use them, another firehouse can."

"Oh this I want to see," Violet mumbled, shaking her head. Stepping forward, she turned to Grant and smiled. "I'll be right back."

"No need. I'll come with you." Moving ahead, he eased between the hulk and the woman he'd just been kissing. He had no idea for sure what Lucy was up to, but he was sure of one thing. He wouldn't give Violet up without a fight.

CHAPTER SEVENTEEN

"**M**an, Cole is one lucky duck." Cole's firefighting buddy Payton polished off his third slice of Lily's chocolate chip banana bread. "I'm going to have to double up on my workout, but it's worth every bite."

Violet was convinced if he hadn't needed to share with his buddy Regan, he would have gladly eaten the entire loaf. "Have you had Lily's mandal bread?"

"Her what?" Payton's brows buckled together.

"Mandal bread. It's like extra baked biscotti."

Now the built fireman outright frowned, shaking his head. "Thought while helping with the new place we'd sampled just about everything Lily bakes, but can't say that I've had the pleasure of trying anything like biscotti."

"Biscotti?" Regan, looked from Payton to Violet. "What's that?"

Both Lucy and Grant, along with Payton, gaped open mouthed at the poor guy.

"What, do you live under a rock?" Payton quipped.

"No sense picking on the poor man." Lucy waved an arm at Payton then turned to his sidekick. "It's an Italian almond biscuit. And even though our Lily doesn't have a drop of Italian blood in her, she nails it every time."

"I bet," the guy agreed. "Everything I've tasted of hers has been out of this world."

Grant reached for a last piece of bread. "That bakery is going to do a bang up business."

"Of course it is," the General boomed from the doorway.

"You're home earlier than we expected, dear." Grams beamed as her husband crossed the room to greet her.

Both firemen quickly wiped their mouths, pushed to their feet and stood at attention. Violet didn't know that much about Cole's firefighting friends, but she'd bet anything both had served in the military. Standing when an officer was on deck was pretty much ingrained in every serviceman.

"At ease," the General said so casually anyone might have thought it was a military barracks and not a family kitchen.

"Guess we should pick up those new plush toys you phoned about." Payton lifted his dish and walked to the sink, his buddy in tow.

"Oh yes," Lucy nodded, "I almost forgot."

"Toys?" Grams asked.

"Stuffed animals for the children. There was a great clearance sale a while back and I remembered the need for more plush toys being mentioned when Cole was convalescing with us. I'd forgotten I had them until today," Lucy explained quickly. Looking down, she weaved around the crowd that had gathered at the island with Lily's baked goods and scurried up the stairs.

To Violet, the woman looked a little too guilty. Then again, ever since she'd tried to set Violet up with the principal's son for prom back in high school, Violet didn't trust Lucy's motives when it came to single men and the Hart granddaughters. Or any other unattached person in the county for that matter.

"With your permission, sir," Payton swiveled to face the General, "we'll go see if we can help."

The General nodded, and the two firefighters hurried after Lucy.

"Sometimes," Grant smiled at the older man, "you really do remind me of my grandfather."

"Yes, well." The General cleared his throat. "Have you given any more thought to the Carter property?"

"Actually, I have." Grant picked up his empty plate turned toward the sink.

At this angle, Violet could see the dimples pit in his cheeks as his lips curved upward. The sight made Violet want to smile back for no good reason.

"And?" The General straightened.

"And," Grant's smile broadened, "we'll need to do some further testing, but if my estimations are correct and the damage isn't catastrophic, this could be a doable project."

The General slapped his hands together and rubbed vigorously.

"That's what I wanted to hear. You may have just made my day, son."

"My pleasure. Now, I'd like you to do something for me."

"You name it."

"I'd like to take you for a ride and show you what F&W can do."

Nodding, the General's smile didn't falter. "Fair enough. When would you like to go?"

Something in the shift of this conversation was making Violet very uneasy. She wasn't quite sure why, but she was positive the universe might be irrevocably shifting.

Flipping his wrist, Grant studied his watch momentarily before looking back at the General. "It's a couple of hours drive, but unless you have other plans, there's no time like the present." He spun about in place and faced Violet. "Would you like to join us?"

"Absolutely." If the rug was about to be pulled out from under her world, she most definitely was coming along for one last ride.

• • • •

Conversation the last couple of hours, from Hart Land to the potential Carter preserve project, had been light and pleasant and entertaining. The General and Violet relayed stories of the granddaughters growing up at the lake. Grant had to admit, considering the founding families' background and current big city life of at least two of the daughters, he had not expected to discover the mothers had been more wannabe hippies than debutants.

He also hadn't expected to be so darn nervous showing the General the latest F&W project. Yes, he wanted to impress the General as a stepping stone to convincing the man that if he sold his property to F&W it would still be well cared for, but more so, he wanted Violet to see this project through his eyes. To see the practical side, as well as the results of all that time spent mulling over the perfect blend of man and nature. "Here we are."

Quietly, the General scanned the perimeter.

Pointing to the six foot chain link fence around the construction site, Grant slowed his car.

Ever since driving onto the property and following the dirt road up to the main building, Grant had kept a close eye on the General and filed his expressions away for future reference. Not that he expected to read much from the stone-faced Marine, but he had hoped to learn anything helpful. Violet, on the other hand, was wide-eyed and tense through the window. He wasn't too proud to admit that he was delighted at her reaction. For the first time in a long time he understood how a rooster or peacock might feel strutting their stuff.

Pulling up to the locked gate, he was surprised the guard was not at the gatehouse.

"Are you expecting to find somebody here?" the General asked.

"Actually, I was. This project is in multiple stages. With anything this large we usually keep a guard as well as locked gates." Grant shrugged. "Maybe he's making his rounds."

Both his passengers nodded. With the sun setting, Grant hadn't expected to find his crew still working. A nearly empty parking lot was no surprise. The one truck no doubt belonged to Larry, the site manager. Since the man would split a nice bonus if they came in ahead of schedule, it made sense he might be working late, but the black sedan parked closer to the facilities building was definitely out of place.

"Unusual car for a construction worker," Violet mumbled almost to herself.

"That's what I was thinking."

In the back seat, the General remained quiet as Grant slid the General's Jeep into a parking space near the maintenance building.

"I want to take a minute and let Larry know we're here. I still feel badly. The previous site supervisor came down with chicken pox shortly after his youngest and we pulled Larry off another project across the state without much notice. He's been a real trooper. Even predicting bringing the project in early."

"Chicken pox?" Violet stepped out of the vehicle. "I didn't think kids got that anymore."

"It still happens. From what I understand, the kid was vaccinated so he got a mild case but my guy never had them as a kid nor did he have the shot, so he's down for the count."

Standing by the car still, the General scanned the area. If Grant didn't know better, he'd almost say the man was still on duty and doing recognizance.

Once the older man had taken in his surroundings, he took an extra few moments to study the nearby parked sedan before facing Grant. "Nice. You left a lot of trees."

It pleased Grant that the General noticed. Taking a step forward, he momentarily forgot about his project manager or the out of place sedan and waved an arm from one side of the lot to the other. "We took extra care not only to remove as few trees as possible, but planted more."

"Even in the parking areas." Now Violet looked around her.

Grant nodded. "We do that with all our projects. At full maturity, not a single car should be exposed to full sun."

"Impressive," the General said.

Yes. Score one for the developers. Grant held the door open for Violet and her grandfather. The building seemed cavernous. Immediately to the right they slipped into the first office. Papers cluttered the tops of the two massive desks. Small stacks of boxes leaned against one wall. At one desk, atop a brown lunch bag, an uneaten sandwich, bag of chips, apple, and bottled soft drink were untouched. The on-the-job meal reminded him more of a grade school lunch than the usual fast food fare seen on a construction site. *Odd.*

"Your site supervisor seems to be AWOL." The General tapped at the desktop, then the brown bag. Finger still tapping, he brought his hand back, dragging the edge of the makeshift placemat a few inches away, and sent the apple rolling to the edge.

Grant scooped the fruit up before it fell to the floor.

"Good save." Violet smiled then quickly frowned. "Did you hear that?"

Listening carefully, Grant waited in silence when what sounded like a muffled cry pierced the silence. "You guys wait here. I'll go take a look."

"I'm coming with you." The General took a step in his direction.

The door slightly open, Grant waved the General and Violet back with one hand, holding the forefinger of the opposite hand against his lips. Something sounding too much like the slapping of a hand against flesh set off his early warning system. Quietly, he inched his way toward the sound, not surprised when the General and Violet followed. He'd made it all of ten or fifteen feet when the source of the noises came into full view, freezing him in place. He blinked once and again, then shook his head. He had to be hallucinating.

The General clasped a hand on Grant's shoulder, holding him in place. As if he had any intention of walking into the sight before him. Arms and legs tied to a hardback chair, his site supervisor, Larry, looked up at a beefy balding hulk who was clearly the source of the slapping sounds. The trickle of blood Grant could see coming down Larry's face didn't look good.

"And what the hell do you expect me to do with toilets?" A few feet back, a man in a dark suit leaned against the wall, arms crossed.

Grant now had a strong suspicion who owned the sedan.

"Do you see signs of anyone besides those two?" the General asked softly, carefully perusing the visible space.

From where they stood, Grant had a decent view of a good portion of the building. Including an impressive stock of boxed toilets. What the hell was going on? No time to figure this out, he pulled out his phone and cursed the lack of bars.

"Violet," he whispered, "there's a landline in the office. Go back, use it to call 911. Then stay low till I come and get you."

For a few long seconds he thought she was going to argue. Nothing had made him as happy as when she nodded her head, mouthed *be careful*, and turned around silently, making her way back to the office and away from danger.

"I'd like to know if there are more of them," Grant mumbled mostly to himself.

The General nodded. "Agreed. I'm going to take a quick spin around the exterior of the building. See how many goons we're dealing with."

While Grant didn't like the idea of putting an old man in a potentially dangerous position, he had to remind himself that this fit as a fiddle *old man* was probably considerably more capable of handling the situation than he was. Filled with reservations, he nodded at the General and crouching low, hugged the wall, inching closer. Now he could see the sheer terror in his supervisor's eyes. Blast.

"They're worth more than the twenty K I owe you."

"Do I look like I'm running a hardware store? We fronted you cash and expect to be paid in cash." Suit guy sounded more agitated.

"I just need a little more time to sell them." His voice catching, Larry swallowed hard. "You've got the five K from what I've already sold off. Just a few more days. That's all I need."

Suddenly all the plumbing issues striking the construction sites were starting to make sense to Grant. If Larry got out of this alive, Grant might want to go a few rounds with the guy himself.

"I've already been patient. Too patient." Suit guy tipped his head at the oversized goon who'd been using his supervisor for a punching bag and walked away.

This could not be good. Grant looked over his shoulder for the General. Relieved not to see Violet coming back, he strained, listening for sirens. Nothing. And then what he deep down knew was coming next raised the stakes.

Bruiser pulled a gun and, standing only feet away from Larry, pointed at his temple. By now Larry had gone from squeaky to balling like a hungry baby.

"Don't do this. I'll cut you in. Seriously. These toilets are worth thousands. Look around this place."

To Grant's surprise, the guy actually looked away. This was his chance. Of all the heavy tools that might have been handy on a construction site, the only thing he had was the stupid apple he'd been holding since the supervisor's first cries caught his attention. Apple? Grant weighed it in his hand. Maybe. It was all he had.

"There's tons of expensive high end shit here." Desperation dripped in the supervisor's voice. "I sell this at a discount, buy the cheaper imports and keep the difference. I'll cut you in. Fifty-fifty."

The big guy wasn't saying anything. He seemed to enjoy watching Larry squirm, or maybe the guy was thinking about it, but Grant couldn't wait any longer. He'd eased as close as he dared. Timing was going to be really tight.

Sucking in a deep breath and offering a silent prayer, Grant wound up for the throw and let the apple rip across the quiet warehouse.

CHAPTER EIGHTEEN

The downside of so many small New England towns was that nothing much ever happened to require any to have a really big police department. Getting help was going to take time. Time Violet was sure they didn't have. She had zero interest in becoming the heroine too stupid to live who ignored instructions and charged in making everything worse for the good guys. On the other hand, crouching on the floor in the office holding onto a handset, peeking through the doorway at nothing, or out the window at the obnoxious sedan, and praying the sheriff and his deputies got here sooner than later wasn't sitting well with her either.

Taking another look at the lone car in the empty parking lot, she wished she had this good a view of the voices growing louder at the other end of the building. Sitting and doing nothing was killing her. She had no idea how much longer this crazy situation was going to last, if the creeps would get away before the cops came, or if Grant and her grandfather were still safe and okay. If only she could…

Tipping her head to one side, she studied the near empty parking lot. Maybe there was something she could do after all.

• • • •

The apple flew out of his hand. Grant would have sworn all the air sucked out of the large room. Like a slow motion movie scene, the green ball cut through the air, following the intended trajectory. Within seconds, the projectile hit its mark. Like David and Goliath, the apple smacked the hulk in the side of the head, and like the biblical giant he fell with a loud thump in one direction. The gun fell to the floor, skidding away.

Grant lunged after the gun before Hulk woke up. A hard green apple tossed at close to 90 miles an hour could do serious damage, but he wasn't taking any chances. Arms out, he slid after the weapon the same way he'd have slid into home plate in a do or die championship game. The only problem was the fingers that curled around the firearm before he could.

"You okay?"

Tracking from the tip of comfortable laced shoes, up a light brown pant leg, all the way to the shit eating grin of the General was better than… well, anything. "Yeah." He pushed to his feet and brushed off his hands. "I'll be better when the cops get here."

"Ditto. Sorry I didn't get back sooner. Found your guard tied up behind some pallets."

"Is he all right?"

"A little shaken up. He's gone to meet the cops at the gate."

Grant glanced at the hulk on the floor and over to his supervisor who had passed out. Whether from pain, injury or fear, Grant didn't have a clue. "I'm going to untie him. Use the ropes to tie this hulk up, then we'll see where his boss went."

"He's leaning against the trunk of his car," the General said, matter of factly. "Yakking away on his cell."

Grant swallowed a groan. Was he the only one on this mountain without cell service?

Doing his best to unknot the ropes at Larry's feet, a low moan drew his attention away, his gaze shooting up to the General firmly pointing the gun at the character on the ground. Grant didn't even want to think how this would have gone down had he been alone and stumbled onto this situation. Another few tugs and pulls and he slid the rope off his employee and turned in time to see Hulk rolling into a sitting position.

"What the…" Hulk rubbed at the side of his head, his eyes widening at the sight of the General holding his gun.

"I'd stay nice and still if I were you." The General's tone remained steady and calm. Even Grant had to admit had he been the one to speak, his voice might have cracked just a smidge.

Hulk laughed. Shaking his head and looking up at the General, he pushed to his feet. "I don't think so, old man."

The sound of the gun cocking came across loud and clear in the quiet room. "Allow me to introduce myself. General Harold Hart, retired, United States Marine Corps."

One leg in motion, Hulk's eyes rounded, his jaw dropped, and he stood frozen in place. Slowly he raised both arms in surrender and set his foot down. The General might as well have announced he was Superman. However stupid Hulk might be, he was smart enough to know, old or not, don't mess with a Marine.

"That's more like it." The General didn't bother to smile, he simply tipped his head toward the ropes in Grant's hands. "Know how to tie him securely?"

Grant nodded. "Always knew making Eagle Scout would come in handy some day." He'd just about gotten the guy's hands secured behind his back when a distant siren broke the silence. *Thank heaven.* Hurrying, he returned to Larry, slowly undoing his hands so he wouldn't fall out of his seat once freed.

The siren grew louder, accompanied by pounding footsteps.

"Don't you hear the sirens? Move…it." Suit came to a halt in the doorway.

Before Grant could blink, the guy's hand was in and out of his jacket. Gun in hand, he and the General looked like a scene from a bad western. Each pointing a lethal weapon at the other.

Suit took a slow step back. "No one wants to die here today." Staring down the General, he retreated another step. "Your man there isn't worth losing your life for."

Cool as a cucumber and steady as the proverbial rock, the General didn't flinch. Keeping his eyes on his target, he dared to move forward a step.

"Now, now." Suit shook his head. "No martyrs today." And in the shadows, he took off toward the parked car.

"We can't let him get away." Grant bolted toward the door, the General half a step ahead.

"I wouldn't worry about that if I were you two." Violet stood where he'd hid earlier and watched the unfolding scene. Something dangling from one hand, she held them up for all to see. "He's not getting very far without these."

The moment the battery connector cables came clearly into view, Grant couldn't stop the laugh that burst from deep in his belly. She'd cut Suit's battery cables. No wonder he loved her. Had he really once considered this woman might be an airhead?

"I couldn't stand by doing nothing. Then it dawned on me, if it worked for the nuns in the *Sound of Music*, why not for me? I was just going to disconnect the cables but thought, nope, needs to be a permanent fix. Didn't hurt that the office desk has some seriously sharp cutting tools."

By the time she got within touching distance, Grant grabbed her hand and curled her into his arms, planting a big kiss on her lips, not caring who saw. "You're amazing."

She giggled under her breath and Grant wanted to kiss her again. "You weren't so bad yourself. I caught most of the show from back there." Her thumb pointed over her shoulder.

"What?" the General shouted to be heard over the sirens that had clearly reached the parking lot. "Don't I count for anything?"

Violet pulled away and slid into her grandfather's embrace, kissing him on the cheek. "You were wonderful too."

Oh hell, was Grant in trouble. He really had it bad for Violet. Why else would he be jealous of kisses for an old man?

● ● ● ●

"I still say the next time you're going to confront the mob, you should bring me along. I know a thing or two about this." Ralph played a card. Most of the night he'd been grumbling and frowning at the General. "A man learns a thing or two working the trains back in the day."

"Ralph," the General lowered his hands to rest on the table, "I did not go looking to confront anyone. Neither Grant nor I had anyway of knowing his supervisor has a gambling problem or that he was into his bookie for over five figures. Shit happens."

"Your language, dear," Fiona Hart said softly. The General sighed, Ralph harrumphed, Thelma rolled her eyes and Grant did his best not to laugh. For most of the evening the only topic of discussion during the impromptu late night card game had been tonight's excitement.

"If you ask me," Lucy came in carrying a tray of snacks, "it's a miracle none of you got yourselves killed."

"I'll admit," Violet came in behind Lucy with her cousins in tow,

"I'd pay big bucks never to be in that situation again."

"You did good cutting off the battery." The General smiled for the first time since sitting down to play.

A huge grin spread across Violet's face. "I am rather proud of myself. I don't know squat about cars except that a car won't go far without a battery."

"He was behind the wheel cussing when the police arrived." Grant played a low card and hoped it was the right move. Things were on a roll today and he didn't want to get on the General's bad side. Even if he had decided not to pursue the purchase of Hart Land. "Foolishly made a break on foot, but not soon enough."

"Are you going to have to testify?" Thelma asked.

Grant shrugged. "If it comes to that."

"Let's hope it doesn't." Ralph sighed as the General scooped up the trick. "The mob can be mean."

"I don't think there's anything to worry about." The General played his next card. "I've spoken with a few people and the victim's statement is enough to get the ball rolling."

"I really hope it ends there." Fiona Hart heaved a deep sigh and poked at her rug. "Nasty business."

"That it is," Ralph agreed.

The General asked over his card. "What's going to happen to the supervisor, Larry?"

"Don't know. Need to talk to my partner. From what I was able to piece together, in over his head, he began selling our high end fixtures and replacing them with inferior product and keeping the profit, but things got out of hand."

Violet set her glass of lemonade on the table beside her. "I guess it's a good thing we walked in on him or this could have gone on for much longer."

"Not likely." Grant shook his head. "My partner Joe has been running around fixing plumbing failures at different projects. This last mess would have brought everything to light sooner than later."

"Wouldn't have minded if it had been sooner." Violet smiled at him. "Chasing after bad guys with guns is best on TV, thank you."

"I propose we shift to a more pleasant subject." Fiona looked up and smiled.

"That would be bedtime for me." Lucy looked around the room. "Anyone need something before I retire?"

A multitude of voices echoed no, thank you, and goodnight. Except Violet. Playing out the last card in the hand, she stood. "It's been a long day and I'm right behind Lucy."

Grant's gaze met Violet's and suddenly he couldn't think of anything more appealing than walking her home. Without skipping a beat, he stood up and laid the last card down. "I'm wiped also, folks."

All he could think of was quickly saying his goodnights and walking Violet to her cabin.

Outside Hart House, Violet paused and took a deep breath. "I think this is one of the lightest winters we've ever had. I'd almost swear spring is around the corner."

"Considering how quickly time passes, I consider anything after the New Year as almost spring." Grant hesitated, waited as she brushed her hands together, blew into them for warmth and then, when her hand fell to her side he slid hers into his and raised the clasping hands up between them. "Do you mind?"

Her lips tipped north and a smile spread across her face. "Not at all. I like it."

"Good, because so do I."

The walk to her cabin was short. Too short. At her door he didn't want to leave. He felt like a teenage kid after a first date. Should he kiss her? Should he be considerate and let her go inside? Should he search for something else to say? Drag the moment on?

Her back to the door, she leveled her gaze with his. "Would you like to come in for some hot chocolate? Or maybe tea?"

Which would take longer to make? "I'd love to. Thank you." Without letting go of her hand, he followed her inside. At some point he knew he'd have to let go. Give her back her hand. But he couldn't bring himself to let go just yet. Still he couldn't hold on to her forever. Slowly he loosened his hold on her hand. "Hot chocolate would be nice if it's not too much trouble."

Easing away from him so slowly, he wondered if maybe she hadn't wanted to lose contact any more than he had. His nephew's favorite song from an old animated movie popped into his mind. He should have just kissed the girl.

He was still standing, rooted to the floor, when she called from the kitchen. "Go ahead and make yourself comfortable. This will only take a minute. Literally. I use the microwave, but don't tell Lucy, she'd have a cow."

"Your secret is safe with me." Biting back a grin, he sank into the comfortable sofa.

"And here we go. I even put little marshmallows on the top. Hope you like them." She handed off one mug and tucking her foot underneath her, sank into the seat beside him.

"Definitely. What's hot chocolate without marshmallows?"

This cabin was definitely more contemporary than his cabin. Besides being much larger, it felt more like a home than a vacation rental. On top of that the view from the sofa was the next best thing to standing on the shore.

"A penny for your thoughts?" She blew on the top of the hot chocolate.

"The view is perfect." And he didn't mean just the shoreline.

Violet sank back into the sofa. "It really is. Every time I'm here, I swear I'll come more often."

"Or just stay?" After such a short time at the lake, ditching the chaos of the real world held much more appeal than it did when he arrived and learned internet was near non-existent.

A cute grin tugged at the corner of her cheeks as she peered over the edge of the mug and out the picture glass window. "I've thought about it."

"Changing your mind about the studio?" His heart dipped low in his chest.

She shook her head. "Not seriously."

"But you've thought about it?"

"For half a second."

"You're sure?"

She sucked in a deep breath that made his heart sink as if he'd hit an air pocket during flight, but she nodded and he felt on even ground again. "Sure."

Before he could say a word, she'd shifted her weight until she was leaning against him, her head tucked into his shoulder. If Violet stayed tucked into his side, if tonight never ended, life—his life—

would be better than good. Maybe his grandfather had a point, remaining a bachelor isn't all it's cracked up to be.

CHAPTER NINETEEN

I f Violet believed in reincarnation, she'd want to come back as a
cat. Sleeping on a porch rocker at Hart House, the new resident
cat, Sadie, yawned, uncurled into a long stretch and then snuggled
back into the cushion. No doubt returning to whatever sweet dreams
cats have.

Inside, the house already buzzed with activity.

"Don't you look all rosy cheeked?" Her sister Heather pulled her
into a tight hug.

Caught by surprise, Violet let out a short squeal. "I didn't know
you were coming."

"Neither did I until late last night. Didn't waste any time, hopped
into my car and bunked in the guest room upstairs. And the best part, I
don't have to be back till Tuesday."

"Morning." Rose, Heather's other sister, stretched like the kitty
on the rocker. "Best night's sleep I've had in ages. I'm starved."

"At least someone got some sleep." Heather flashed Rose a
cheesy grin. "Now I know what people mean by snoring like a freight
train."

"I do not." Rose reached around Heather to hug Violet. "Boy,
has the lake air done you good."

"She does look…" Heather searched for words.

Cindy came in from the kitchen carrying a large dish of Lucy's
buttermilk pancakes. "Try in love."

"What?" Like a pair of matching bobble heads, Rose and
Heather snapped around, gaping at their cousin.

Cindy shrugged. "Maybe infatuated, but my money's on love."

"What?" the two sisters echoed again, this time spinning around
to look at Violet.

"Don't look at me that way." Shaking her head, she glared at her
cousin Cindy. "The woman is delusional."

"No she isn't." Carrying a platter of bacon, Poppy came in

behind her sister Cindy. "And he's in love too. Though I'm not sure he knows it yet."

"Good grief." Heather hefted her hands onto her hips. "You come home for one lousy week and fall in love? Who does that?"

"You!" Four voices, including Callie who had just come in the door, shouted in unified synchronization.

"Yeah, well." A sly grin slid across Heather's face. Violet loved how happy her sister looked since falling for Jake. Not that Heather had ever looked unhappy before. Mostly she was tired and overworked, standard operating procedure for a doctor, but now she always had a twinkle in her eyes.

Was that what Violet's family saw in her? Did her eyes twinkle? Were they all correct? Could she be falling in love? Because she sure did feel like walking on a cloud. And every time she thought about Grant going his separate way, her stomach did an obnoxious flip that made her want to curl over and grip her gut.

"Whatever you girls are jawing over can wait." Lucy carried her crowd-pleasing French toast casserole. "If you want your breakfast warm, you'd better get moving. The General and your grandmother are already inside drinking coffee with Mr. Whitaker."

And this was why her cousins thought she was in love. She knew she was grinning like the cat that swallowed the canary. The tug of her cheeks was so strong her face almost hurt. And she couldn't help any of it. The anticipation of sitting down to breakfast with Grant, of hopefully spending the rest of the day together, had her happier than when she'd learned her studio would be saved, and giddier than back in high school when the star of the football team asked her to prom. *Oh hell*. They were right. Now what?

• • • •

Grant's thoughts had been running a mile a minute. He'd taken more days than he should and like it or not, he needed to be at the office tomorrow.

"Ah, my girls." The General pushed to his feet and out of sheer habit, Grant followed suit.

A parade of attractive women filed into the room. He recognized

Callie, Cindy, and Poppy, but the striking redhead and another blonde were unfamiliar to him. Not that it mattered, the only face that had his heart doing an Irish jig was Violet. Damn, he didn't want to leave tomorrow.

One by one, each woman gave the General a kiss on the cheek then stepped over and did the same with their grandmother.

"You haven't met my other granddaughters, Grant." The General waved toward the redhead. "This is Rose, Violet's sister."

Rose waved on her way to the buffet sideboard.

"And this is Heather—"

"My other sister." Violet cut her grandfather off. "You met her fiancé at the hardware store."

Grant nodded. "That's right. Nice to meet you."

"Same here." Heather smiled.

"She still lives in Boston," the General continued. "But as soon as the new cardiac care wing is built at our hospital, she'll be close to home again."

Now waiting her turn at the sideboard, Heather blew out a slow sigh. "Can't happen soon enough. Ground breaking is in a few weeks."

From there, the line formed at the buffet where the second round of breakfast fare was spread out. He and the Harts had enjoyed the first round, and even though he'd eaten his full, he stood for seconds and the chance to stand by Violet. Lady, or was it Sarge, rose from beside the General and followed him. "Sleep well?" he asked softly.

"Mm. Very." She reached for a plate, sidestepping the other dog.

"I do believe this will be the first Sunday supper in a very long time that all three Preston girls will be joining us." Fiona grinned sweetly, dabbing the corners of her mouth with a napkin. "Rose, how did you manage to escape?"

"A shipment from the upcoming Egypt exhibit got delayed in arrival due to off season storms and then tangled up in customs." Carrying a dish loaded with enough food to feed a man twice her size, Rose headed for the empty seat beside Grant, bumped against a golden retriever and stepped aside taking the seat next to her grandmother instead.

Good dog.

"No point in watching my blood pressure rise waiting for it to clear," Rose continued. "When Heather phoned she was coming up, I hitched a ride."

"And we're so happy you did." Fiona Hart had a smile that could light a room. And from what Grant could see, all the granddaughters inherited it. "What about you, Heather? It's been a few weeks since you broke away."

Heather stabbed at a pancake with a large serving fork and plopped it atop another already resting on her plate. "I'm still not sure how it happened, but my surgical schedule is clear till Wednesday morning." The other dog escorted her to the table, nudging her toward two empty seats the way he might if she were vision impaired.

"Well," the General set his coffee mug down, "whatever brings my girls home is fine with me."

"Good morning." The man Grant had met at the hardware store came hurrying in. The wave of his hand seemed to be in salutation for the room, but his eyes were on one woman, and the broad smile that spread across his face was clearly meant for only Heather. Eyes locked, he took the empty seat beside her and below the table two hands quickly linked.

Grant had seen plenty of happy couples in his lifetime, but he was pretty sure if they didn't look away soon the heat in their gaze might be enough to set the whole room on fire. Despite Heather's claims to not knowing how it happened, Grant suspected the reason for the three day break in her schedule had just sat down beside her. A short bark and a tail thump, the dog trotted back to the line at the buffet.

What he now recognized as Violet's ring tone sounded.

"Sorry." She set her plate down on the sideboard. "I'm expecting an important call about my studio." Smiling quickly at him, she hurried from the room and stood just outside the doorway.

Placing a few token items on his plate, Grant retook his seat, doing his best to listen in over the hungry clatter of silverware and the animated conversation in the dining room. According to Heather, the new cardiac wing would be in construction for about a year. Fiona hoped they weren't planning on waiting that long for a wedding. And it sounded like Violet agreed to meet with the design team the next morning.

"Good news, dear?" Fiona Hart slid her knife and fork closed as her granddaughter entered the room.

"Yes. I'm meeting with the architect and engineer at ten thirty." Quickly Violet served herself some eggs and wheat toast and hurried to take the seat beside Grant. "The man I spoke with sounded very nice and already seemed to have a good handle on what I need as well as eager to have me up and running soon."

"Stan's a good man." Grant nodded before realizing what he'd just said.

Violet's fork hit the plate. "Did I mention his name?"

"Uh…" Grant scrambled for a way to get his foot out of his mouth. Nothing was coming to mind.

A deep crease formed between Violet's brows. "I did not."

The General cleared his throat and directed his words to Grant. "You're welcome to use my office if you would like."

"Yes sir. Thank you." Grant pushed to his feet and extended a hand to Violet. "If you wouldn't mind coming with me. I have something to explain."

Lips pressed tightly together, for a few moments it looked as though Violet would refuse. Air filled his lungs again when she nodded and led the way out of the dining room.

He'd taken two steps into the room when she closed the door behind them and whirled about to face him. "You got one of your investors to buy my building, didn't you?"

"Not exactly." Hooking his hand around the back of his neck, Grant contemplated the best words for what he wanted to say. From the fire burning in her gaze, he wasn't sure any words would do.

Violet crossed her arms. "Then exactly what?"

Like yanking a Band-Aid off, fast and to the point was probably best. "I bought the building."

"You?" Violet's eyes rounded wide.

He nodded. "With the name of your studio it wasn't hard to find the property address or track down the owner."

"Why?" Incredulity stared back at him. He supposed that was better than anger.

Sucking in a fortifying breath, he took a step in her direction. "I would think that was obvious."

"Considering how much work the building needs, and that I'm getting a whole new studio, and that my rent is not going up, it doesn't sound like a very sound investment."

"It's not a bad investment. It's a good neighborhood."

She moved a step closer to him. "Not bad, but not good?"

"More like delayed return."

Her brow buckled with confusion. "I may prefer the simpler things in life: a fire on the beach, watching the sunset at Eagle Point, or Sunday supper with the family, but I'm a banker's daughter. Either the math works or it doesn't."

"Some things are more important than math." He inched forward.

"Or money?"

He nodded and took the last step bringing him in front of her. "Or money."

Violet blinked. He could see the wheels turning in her head. What he didn't know is what conclusion she was coming to. Not realizing until this very second how much it would hurt if she turned and walked away, he carefully placed his hands on her forearms, slid them down along each arm, and folded his hands around hers.

"I don't get it," she muttered.

"I suppose it's rather simple. Some things are more important than making money." After coming face to face at the warehouse with a life threatening situation, he'd finally learned what really mattered most. Not the toilets or his business or making money—Violet.

Her brows rose high on her forehead and his heart kick started when her fingers linked with his and she smiled. "So, what you're saying is there's a balance to life?"

"Yeah." He nodded. "I guess I am."

"So the lake worked its magic on you."

He shook his head. "Not the lake."

Again, that confused crinkle appeared on her forehead.

"You did."

Eyes rounded, circling those beautiful cobalt eyes in a white rim.

He tugged her close against him and gently pressed a brief sweet kiss to her lips. Still close enough to feel her warm breath on his face, he squeezed her hands. "I don't think I could handle losing you."

"You don't?" Her voice sounded barely above a whisper.

Shaking his head, he muttered just as softly, "I don't."

An easy smile bloomed. "Good."

"Good?" Now he felt confused.

"Because I don't want to lose you either."

Letting go of her hands, he slid his arms around her waist, delighted when she looped hers around him. "We have an office in Boston."

"You do?" her smile widened.

He nodded. "And there's this new project I've taken on that's going to keep me there for a while."

"There is?" She tightened her hold on him.

His breath caught for a moment at her nearness. "Is it too soon to mention I love you?"

"Probably." She smiled. "But don't let that stop you."

"I love you, Violet Preston."

Violet's lips fell too briefly on his before she tilted her head back and stared up at him. "And I love you."

Grant held back a knowing chuckle. "I think very soon we're going to make my grandfather a very happy man."

"Your grandfather?"

"For years he's encouraged me to find a good woman and settle down. Wait till he finds out I found a great woman."

Violet giggled.

"What's so funny?"

"Considering it's his fault you're here at all, I just thought it funny that we found each other." Violet brushed her hand against his brow. "You're frowning. Change your mind about me already?"

He squeezed her tight. "Not on your life. You're stuck with me."

A bark sounded from the doorway. Sitting like a couple of sentinels, Sarge and Lady wagged their tails in contented synchronization.

"Life doesn't get much better than this." Violet smiled up at him.

Running his fingers through her hair, he leveled his gaze with hers. "You ain't seen nothing yet."

CHAPTER TWENTY - EPILOGUE

"**T**his has to be the absolute best party I have ever, in my entire life, been to." Louise Franklin, the town's biggest gossip and ring leader of the unofficial Merry Widows Club, bit into one of Lily's fudge brownies and moaned loud enough that Iris covered her mouth to hide her grin.

"To think, we can have any of Lily's end-of-the-world delicious baked goods twenty-four seven." Thelma, owner of the antique store and another member of the Merry Widows, even though her husband Nate was alive and well, shoved a spitzbuben cookie into her mouth and Iris could almost see the woman's eyes roll back into her head behind closed lids.

"Twenty-four seven may be a bit of an exaggeration." Lily looked over the display counter that only a couple of hours ago had been brimming with freshly baked goods for this pre-opening fete. "For sure we're closing on Sunday afternoons and probably Mondays too. As for twenty-four hours, well folks will have to make due with the bakery closing at six."

"Isn't this just great?" Violet sidled up beside her cousin. "The place looks fantastic."

Zinnia, Iris' sister, inched closer. "I think every soul in town is here."

"No one wanted to miss the pre-opening party," Violet said, all the while her eyes tracking the room until landing on the tall guy in casual clothes and, of course, Italian shoes.

The grin that lit up Violet's face, and her eyes, made Iris want to smile too. "I see he's still wearing leather shoes at the lake."

Violet blinked, her smile momentarily slipping before the dawn of understanding hit and her face lit up again. "Oh, well. Some things are just meant to be."

"I suppose that's true." It certainly was for Violet and Grant. Anyone within a five mile radius could feel the heat generated by the two even while standing across the room from each other. Any minute now Iris almost expected Cole, Lily's fiancé, to have to step in with a fire extinguisher.

"I think it was a brilliant idea having this…" Poppy looked to her cousins, "easy opening exclusively for the town."

"Soft," Lily corrected, joining her cousins. "Zinnia was the one who came up with the idea, insisting it would help build anticipation for residents in neighboring towns."

"And," Zinnia waved a finger at her cousin, "you'll see I'm right the next time these doors open for business."

"No one can ever say you lack confidence." Iris pulled her sister into a quick hug. "I love you."

"Back at ya!" Zinnia grinned and winked at Lily.

"Yeah, yeah," Lily teased the two sisters and gestured to the bakery still almost brimming with people mulling about. "The question now is how do we politely get rid of everyone and get home for supper?"

"I'll tell the General," Violet volunteered. The fact that the General stood across the room next to Grant, whose attention was equally invested in Violet rather than the men chatting around him, might have had just a teeny bit to do with her eagerness to float across the bakery.

"That'll do it," Lily chuckled.

As predicted, across the room in record time, Violet laid a hand on the General's arm, said a few words, then leaned into Grant. The man's arm looped around her waist and adoring eyes locked on her for so long Iris' heart swelled with joy and ached at the same time. Despite her parent's and grandparent's happy marriages, years of working for the ultra rich had tainted Iris' views on happily ever after. It was nice to be reminded that unlike VHS players and rotary phones, love hadn't become obsolete. At least for some.

"May I have your attention please." The General used his commanding officer tone. "It's about time for the family to head home for supper, but my granddaughter would like to say a few words first."

"Isn't it something," Poppy's head moved from side to side in slow wonder, "how all that man has to do is say is he's ready to leave and everyone almost instinctively follows?"

"Yep," Iris agreed. "Guess that's why he got his stars."

Already, as Lily gave her thank yous for coming and spreading the word about the public grand opening in two days, one by one the folks in attendance moved about the bakery slipping uneaten goods into small white paper bags emblazed with The Pastry Stop and tossed their plastic plates into one of the trash cans. By the time she finished her very brief speech thanking the town, the fire department and her family, the place was empty, relatively cleaned up, and all of the Hart family were ready to go home and continue celebrating the big day. After all, a big day for any member of the clan was a big day for everyone.

"Considering how much food was consumed, I'm really surprised there's so much left over." Poppy carried the last cake tray to the back of Iris' car.

"Which is why it's all going to Hart House. I have a feeling supper today may turn into extended desserts!" Iris laughed, opening the car door.

All it took was about fifteen minutes to have the dessert banquet set up on the buffet and everyone seated nibbling on their favorite leftover confection.

Cindy raised a mini cannoli as though toasting with champagne. "I say we make dessert first the new standard for family suppers!"

"While I think that's a great idea," Poppy nodded to her sister, "I don't think my hips will agree."

"Just remember," Lucy stood in the doorway carrying in a large bowl of salad, "there's pot roast with my special spinach casserole."

Iris smiled at the chorus of moans. Only Lucy could make a spinach casserole worthy of competition with Lily's cannolis.

"How was India?" Cindy popped a forkful of white chocolate cake in her mouth.

"Ah." It was Iris' turn to moan. "That's a story for another day."

Zinnia waved a fork at her sister before stabbing at a cheesecake bite. "And probably the root of her new job."

"Yes. When do you start the new position?" the General asked.

"Monday. The Beltons seem very nice. I'm so looking forward to a normal work week schedule."

"And more weekends at the lake," Her grandfather casually tacked the declaration onto Iris' words.

"And more time at the lake," Iris agreed with a smile. She really was looking forward to being with family. It never got old how close the cousins had managed to stay through adulthood. She only hoped this continued as one by one the women all seemed to be bringing a new dynamic of men into the family fold.

So far the large dining room and table had easily accommodated the three soon-to-be family members.

"Are those your scalloped potatoes?" Jake Harper, holding hands with Heather, followed Lucy into the dining room.

"It is." She set the dish onto a matching buffet that had been purchased to accommodate the increasing dinner crowd.

"You're killing us with calories, Lucy," Cole teased. Also holding his fiancée's hand, the two strolled into the room behind Heather and Jake.

Iris smiled, amused that the two couples took a surprisingly longer time to arrive at the house than the rest of the clan. Except, looking around she realized Violet and Grant were still not in attendance. And they were the first to leave the bakery. What was that all about?

"Do we have any wedding dates set yet?" The General was not one to beat around the bush.

Both couples cast furtive glances at each other, grinning like a couple of besotted teens.

Heather cleared her throat. "As a matter of fact, we've decided waiting for the new wing to be complete is too long. So we're looking at a date for this summer."

"So are we!" Lily's voice oozed excitement.

From the way that folks popped up from their seats hugging and whooping, the scene was reminiscent of the excitement when each got engaged. Except for the General. The man nodded his smiling approval, but his current broad grin was directed to a distant point out the window.

Iris followed his gaze and spotted what had caught his attention. So enthralled in the new wedding announcements, none of the other cousins noticed the couple standing out on the point. Funny how as the two faced each other, holding both hands, only inches apart, even from this distance, Iris could feel the love coming off the pair in waves.

Grant's head tipped forward and the simple act of leaning his forehead against Violet's filled Iris with a sweet warmth and just a hint of longing. About to look away and give her cousin the privacy she deserved, Grant slowly lowered and Iris swallowed a gasp.

Down on one knee, he pulled one hand away from her and fished what had to be a ring from his breast pocket. She had no idea what he was saying, but considering he remained frozen like a statue, it had to be more than 'marry me'. Violet's head bobbed up and down and then the ring slipped onto her finger, Grant stood, and Violet threw her arms around his neck. Like a scene from a romantic movie of old, Grant spun her around before letting her slide to her feet and planting a kiss worthy of a Hollywood blockbuster.

Turning her attention back to the crowd in the room, she noticed her grandfather. Grinning like the Cheshire cat, he too had found it time to turn away. So much happiness. So much to celebrate. All reminding her how once upon a time the only things she'd wanted out of life was the love of a good man and a cozy home filled with children. When had she stopped waiting for a family of her own?

From Lily's Recipe Box

CHOCOLATE CHIP BANANA BREAD

What you'll need:

½ cup salted butter (1 stick)
1 cup sugar
2 eggs
3 ripe bananas, mashed
1 1/3 cup flour
2/3 cup oats
1 teaspoon baking soda
¼ tsp salt
1 cup chocolate chips
½ cup nuts (optional)

Instructions:

Cream butter & sugar.
Beat in eggs and bananas.
Mix dry ingredients and add to banana mixture just until moistened.
Do NOT over mix.
GENEROUSLY GREASE loaf pan(s).

Yields:
One: 9 x 5 inch loaf pan - Bake at 350 degrees for 55-60 minutes.
Three: 5 ¾ x 3 x 2 inch pans – Fill about 2/3 full - Bake at 350 degrees for 45 minutes

Note: Always preheat oven to desired temperature

Excerpt from IRIS

Elephants are majestic animals. A long list of adjectives popped into Iris' head. Huge being at the top, followed by enormous—no, make that ginormous. Next would be powerful, and as the animal in question lifted his trunk up high in the air blowing out a deafening sound that bore an unbearable resemblance to an off-key tuba, the word petrifying beat out all the others.

"Iris," a voice called from the thatched greenery behind her.

She really hadn't wanted to accompany the Throckmortons to India. Her parents had told her dreadful things about the weather, the crowds, the food, and assorted unpleasantries. On the other hand, romantic childhood images of the Taj Mahal and devoted princes urged her to be more adventurous. Get out of her comfort zone. Away from the big cities. Anyone could shop the Champs Elysee in Paris, but to ride an elephant in India?

The elephant stomped closer, shaking the ground beneath her feet at the same time the voice called a little louder. It was the touch of the giant beast's trunk on her shoulder that had her voice tearing from deep in her lungs.

"Miss Iris," another voice screeched almost as loudly.

It took Iris a few seconds to realize she was no longer in India, or Thailand, or Timbuktu for that matter. She no longer worked for the Throckmortons, and the poor woman she'd just scared half to death was the Belton's new housekeeper. "Sorry."

Now halfway across the room, standing frozen in place like a petrified tree trunk, the shaken woman managed to exhale a barely controlled breath. "You said not to let you nap more than an hour."

Iris glanced at the clock on her nightstand. Yes. Sleeping had been difficult. Ever since her run in with that all too playful elephant on that last trip, her nights had been restless and filled with worst case scenarios. Not even changing jobs, taking the prospect of distant travel and spoiled full-blown teenagers off the table, had helped. "Thank you, Ella. I'll be downstairs momentarily."

"Also, Master Michael phoned. He's been invited to dinner at the Carmichael's. What shall I tell him?"

Running the list of acceptable companions and invitations the Beltons had left her, she clearly remembered the Carmichaels were at the top of the yes-by-all-means list. "That will be fine."

Wringing her hands, Iris shook her head and blew out a sigh. The Belton's daughter Tiffany would be home soon. Then the battles would ensue. Homework first, girl talk second. More than once Iris had come close to burning the pre-teen's cell phone in effigy to whoever had actually invented the blasted thing. The privileged daughter had been helicoptered her entire life. Who was Iris kidding, the girl was just plain spoiled rotten, and Iris doubted any amount of restricted parenting at this point could turn that around. Tiffany would no doubt become one of those uppity society mothers more than ready to raise another generation of self-absorbed children who would grow up to believe everything in life could be resolved with a signature at the bottom of a check. Any delusions Iris may have had that she could make a difference in these pre-teens lives had pretty much come and gone as swiftly as her nightmares.

"Would you like a cup of tea?"

Lost in her own thoughts, Iris hadn't even noticed Ella had remained watching her. The fear in the housekeeper's voice had shifted to concern in her eyes. More than one night, Ella had come into the kitchen when she should have been sleeping because she'd heard Iris making tea. "That would be nice, thank you."

Her cell phone beeped and the familiar number brought a smile to her face. "Hello, General."

"You still sound…tired."

Her grandfather was the most imposing man she knew, and yet she loved him with all her heart. "Have I said thank you lately?"

"Thank you?" The gruff voice faltered in confusion.

"For raising Mom and my aunts like normal people and making sure all of us kids did normal things and grew up level headed and well—"

"Normal," he repeated. "Yes, you have. But I can't take the credit for that. If your grandmother had let me have my way, you'd all have grown up with revelry, mess call, and lights out. Could have been like boot camp." The last part came out sort of wistful and made Iris smile.

The man had indeed tried to impose early to bed and early to rise rules on his granddaughters and every so often even on his guests, but their Grams had indeed kept things blissfully unmilitary. "Then thank you for marrying Grams."

The bluster in the old man's voice made her laugh out right. She wasn't sure she'd ever heard the man be in anything except utter and complete control.

"Yes. Well. About you coming to the lake," he sputtered.

How could she have forgotten? Working as a nanny for New York's upper crust, she'd done her share of traveling. The Throckmortons, however, had upped the concept of travel a notch. The family had her traipsing around every nook and cranny of the world while homeschooling their two children. Not that they ever really had a home, more a house for the season. She hadn't minded at first, but as the cute children sprouted into disrespectful self-absorbed teenagers, the job had grown tiresome. India was the last straw. Not to mention, despite her best efforts, those same cell phone addicted teens had developed an attitude of entitlement where they'd begun to look down at her as mere hired help. That made Iris laugh. She could match her education and pedigree notch for notch with the best families on the New York social register, she just didn't see any reason to. Working for the Beltons was supposed to be more of a nine to five, Monday through Friday arrangement, allowing her more time to visit her family on the lake. She missed more time with her cousins. Their lives were moving on and she was beginning to feel a bit left out. In the weeks she'd been at the Briar Cliff estate, the children had been left solely in her care more often than not. There could be no taking even an afternoon off, never mind escape for a weekend to the lake. Like it or not, she was seriously over being responsible for other people's children. "Things aren't working out the way I'd hoped."

"Young lady, you were very clear. This latest governess job would be strictly weekdays only."

She stifled a giggle. No one used the word governess anymore. "As I said, things haven't worked out as planned. Mr. Belton has had to extend his business dealings in London and Mrs. Belton has seen fit to join him."

"Perhaps if they didn't have someone as competent as you to rely on, the mother would return to her post and do her duty."

Yes, Iris would get right on explaining to Abigail Smythe Belton how she needed to come home and do her duty. Iris glanced out the window. Although. "You know, sir, that may not be a bad idea at all."

Now all she had to do was enlighten her newest employer that the General always knew best.

•　•　•　•

This was the right decision. The right thing to do. Definitely the right thing. Glancing at the rearview mirror at the two young children in the back seat, Eric Johnson prayed this was the right thing to do. If it weren't, he was just plain out of ideas.

The moping four year old little boy clutched at the stuffed leopard backpack and shifted his gaze from the window to the front seat. "Are we here yet?"

"Almost."

Hart House couldn't be close enough. The same question had been asked and answered multiple times in the last thirty minutes. Just ahead, to the side of the road, a huge sign with a lake vista background covered in large neon white letters declared Welcome to Lawford. The vise that had been squeezing his heart for the last few hours, a painful reminder this was his last hope, eased slightly. According to the GPS, the rambling white house, literally pretty as a picture, should be just around the bend. His only connection to the past and the future had been the cheery card he'd come across confirming the reservation for another perfect family getaway.

Perched deep into the wooded lot, the rambling Victorian house boasted a wrap around front porch that invited a weary traveler to sit down, take a load off his feet, and indulge in a cool beverage, almost whispering you made the right choice. Nothing could have made a prettier sight. Well, maybe Adele waving madly with a bright smile across her face.

The circle drive seemed to cut the property in sections. Elevated on a slight hill sat the welcoming house. Opposite the drive, patches of green grass dotted with small white cabins cascaded down the hillside to the lake. Any other time and he would have simply taken in the splendid view. The postcard hadn't exaggerated.

"I want to go home." The little boy frowned, strangling his stuffed backpack. His only comfort.

As expected, the stubborn cry had wakened his sleeping sister. Almost two years older, Emily blinked quickly, looked left then right, and for a split-second Eric thought he saw a spark of contentment in her eyes before she silently turned to her brother and softly whispered, "Me too."

"You're here!" The loud, enthusiastic call startled Eric away from the sad sight in the rearview mirror.

"We've been waiting." A grinning middle-aged woman in a gingham dress reminiscent of something Andy Taylor's aunt would have worn, clapped her hands together. "My, how you've grown."

Beside the friendly greeter trotting in their direction, a sleek woman with shoulder length gray hair practically glided down the stairs and flashed a photo perfect smile. "Oh, my Lucy, I think you're right." Even wearing a bright blue and orange flowing floor length dress, she reminded him of royalty. Her face could have easily been the inspiration for a hundred ancient statues.

The first woman, Lucy, swung the rear door open before he could fully escape from the car. She looked to Emily. "I have peanut butter cookies fresh out of the oven."

This time he was sure a flash of delight flickered in his niece's eyes. He'd have to make a note. Emily liked peanut butter cookies.

"And you, young Mr. Gavin," she turned, smiling at the frowning boy, "chocolate chip with M&Ms for you."

The frown slipped and a smile most definitely pursed the child's lips for a full five seconds before he remembered he wanted to go home.

"Come on now," the woman clapped her hands, "can't let the cookies get cold."

Though still not smiling, neither child complained. To Eric's surprise, they'd unbuckled their safety belts, scrambled out of the car and each taking hold of a proffered hand, followed the woman up the stairs. The almost too-friendly woman continued talking as though this was the happiest day in anyone's life, including the two silent children.

"It takes time."

He'd forgotten about the other lady.

"I'm Fiona Hart." She extended her hand.

"Pleased to meet you." He stole a quick look at the now empty porch stairs. "I gather those are the children's favorite cookies?"

"They are." The woman nodded. "Or at least they were when they stayed here last year. Lucy didn't mention it, but she made fresh sweet lemonade too. The children loved it during their last visit."

He nodded, not convinced Gavin was old enough to remember, but hopeful the flicker of light in Emily's eyes meant she did. "I know so little."

"The same can be said for parents of newborns. No one is handed a child with instructions. It will come together." Her hand landed on his forearm.

For the first time since that horrible phone call, Eric thought maybe she might be right. He looked to the back of the car and wondered if it would be all right to check in and take the luggage to their cabin or if he should wait to do that later and follow the children instead.

"They'll be fine with Lucy if you'd like to check in. My husband will come and get your bags."

Eric didn't mean to let his surprise show, but at the chuckle the lovely woman failed to suppress, he must have looked very surprised. Not that he meant any offense, but the woman was most definitely old enough to be his... mother's older sister.

"Career military. The man could probably still march a fifty pound pack across Camp LeJeune in the dead of summer during a hunger strike."

"Make that one hundred pounds." Flanked by a dog at each side, a tall man with a full head of white hair and broad shoulders that shouted they'd done more than their share of work, appeared behind him and shoved his hand at him. "General Hart."

Despite his current civilian status, Eric was overcome with the urge to salute.

"This is the young man we were discussing," his wife said softly.

"Oh, yes." The man's booming voice lowered, the bright smile slipped. "Awfully sad business, all of that."

Awfully sad about covered it. As if confirming the consensus, one of the dogs stepped forward with one paw, stretched his neck and licked Eric's hand. He almost felt like smiling.

The General gave his dog a pat of approval and tipped his chin in his wife's direction. "You go with Fiona and she'll get you the keys."

"Under the circumstances, we thought it best to have you in a cabin closer to the main house. You'll still have the lovely view." Fiona waved him on. Eric hesitated, looking toward the back of the new SUV he'd bought. The General seemed to be hauling out the bags as if they were filled with feathers. By the time Eric turned back, Fiona was up the stairs and at the front door. He'd had to take the steps two at a time to catch up.

Inside, the main house was everything the exterior implied. Large dark wood pieces from centuries past took up space against light airy walls. Vases filled with fresh flowers shared space with bowls of fruits and colorful dishes of assorted candies.

Fiona made her way into the parlor, opened the drawer on a massive partners' desk and handed him a key. "Here you go."

"Don't I have to sign anything?"

"Why?" She smiled. "You're here, aren't you?"

"Well, uhm. Thank you." He supposed that was one way to look at it. He was indeed here and he had given his credit card number online. But for the first time since finding himself lost and confused, like Alice in Wonderland suddenly in a bizarre and unfamiliar world, he dared to hope this other worldly place might be his salvation.

Available at your favorite bookseller.

MEET CHRIS

USA TODAY Bestselling Author of more than a dozen contemporary novels, including the award-winning *Champagne Sisterhood*, Chris Keniston lives in suburban Dallas with her husband, two human children, and two canine children. Though she loves her puppies equally, she admits being especially attached to her German Shepherd rescue. After all, even dogs deserve a happily ever after.

More on Chris and her books can be found at
www.chriskeniston.com

Follow Chris on Facebook at ChrisKenistonAuthor
or on Twitter @ckenistonauthor

Questions? Comments?
I would love to hear from you.
You can reach me at chris@chriskeniston.com

www.ingramcontent.com/pod-product-compliance
Lightning Source LLC
Chambersburg PA
CBHW030638190726
48286CB00008B/2564